Her New Year's Wish

Tia Marlee

A NOVEL CHOICE PRESS

Book Cover by German Creative

Edited by Lia Huntington

Proofread by Jammom Reads

To those whose dreams seem far off.
Never stop wishing for them to come true!

Contents

CHAPTER ONE

Anne

THE END OF NOVEMBER

THE SMELL OF HAIR dye and shampoo tickles my nose when I unlock the front door to the salon and step inside. I set my bag behind the counter, flip on all the lights, and turn the door sign to open. Once that's settled, I move the big rug in front of the door to catch the snow and slush off people's shoes as they enter. The snowstorms this week have dumped just enough to be an inconvenience, but not enough to keep clients at home.

Running the only hair studio in town can be exhausting, especially since Piney Brook seems to be growing overnight into more than a small stop along the way to the bigger city of Bentonville. I grab the lint roller and roll off the cat hair Shelby left behind on my pants this morning, then fetch my apron from the hook and slip it over my head.

Once I'm presentable, I grab the towels from the dryer and start folding them. My first appointment isn't for another thirty minutes, so I let my mind get lost in the task. The soft music floating through the speakers gives me something to sing along to while my hands are busy.

"Hello?" A deep voice cuts through my thoughts, startling me, and I drop the towel I was folding.

I snag the towel from the ground before turning toward the door. A shiver runs through me when I get a good look at the person who interrupted my few minutes of morning peace. "Hudson! You scared me. What brings you in so early?"

He grins and runs his hands through his shaggy hair. The ends curl up over his collar and lay over his ears. "I thought I'd see if you could squeeze me in for a cut before work this morning. Dad said I'm looking like Shaggy from Scooby Doo."

Am I hallucinating, or is he blushing a little? I should have had more coffee. I knew skipping that second cup was a mistake. Glancing at the clock on the wall, I see I still have twenty minutes before Mrs. Willowby's here for her weekly appointment. "Sure, have a seat." I move the basket of towels off the chair and motion for him to sit.

"Thanks." He's more serious than I've seen him be. Though, to be fair, I haven't spent a ton of time with him alone. Maybe he's just not a morning person, or maybe he's only charming in a crowd.

He flirted mercilessly with me at Heath's birthday party, but didn't ask me out, so I assume he's just a friendly, outgoing guy. Especially since every time we hang out with Heath and Gabby, he's a shameless flirt. I flirt back to be friendly, but I can't imagine it going any further than that. According to Heath, he's the type to never settle down, and I'm not interested in dating just to date. The next man I go out with will be marriage material. At least, I hope so. I'm getting too old to keep wasting my time. I want marriage and a family. Someone to come home to at the end of the day.

"No problem. What are you thinking?" I listen as Hudson describes the type of cut he usually gets. "So, a classic fade with a medium-length slick back on top?" I ask to confirm. "I can do that."

"So," he says, as I wrap the cape around his broad shoulders. "How've you been?"

"Good. It's been busy with everyone getting ready for the holidays and stuff. What about you?" I grab the clippers and the number two guard from my drawer and get started bringing the sides back into shape.

"Oh. You know . . . busy as ever." He shrugs. "We finished up the Coffee Loft job and went right to the next job site. A vet's office, which will be nice, but the perks aren't as good as working right next to a coffee shop."

I grin. "I bet Lacey and Aurora are thrilled. It's all the moms have been talking about when they come in. From what I hear, their businesses are booming." Setting down the clippers, I grab my comb and scissors and get to work on the top.

"I think they are. I can't even grab a coffee in the morning anymore without waiting in a huge line." He smiles at me through the mirror. "Are you ready for Christmas?"

Small talk is awkward for most people, but I'm used to it. Customers like to chat while they get their hair done, and my job is to make them comfortable, so they keep coming back instead of driving somewhere else. "Nope," I say, popping the p. "I haven't even started."

"I rarely start until the weekend before Christmas." He chuckles. "I never know what to get anyone."

"Me either," I say. "Thankfully, the girls get together and watch Christmas movies and share cookies and treats. So that's not too hard. I really just shop for my parents."

"Yeah. It's just me and Dad, so I don't need to get much either."

He goes quiet, lost in his own thoughts, so I don't interrupt until I'm finished. "You're all set," I say, brushing the loose hairs off his neck. "Unless you see something you want me to change?"

"No, it looks great. Thanks."

I remove his cape and follow him to the register to ring him up. "Well, thanks for coming in," I say, handing him back his card.

"It was good to see you again." He slides the card back into his wallet. "I . . . Well, I better go." He turns on his heel and beats feet for the door.

That was weird.

The door opens again, letting in a gust of cold air. "Mrs. Willowby, good to see you." She takes off her overcoat and drapes it across her arm. "Give me just one moment to clean up my station, and I'll be ready for you."

"Take your time, dear," she says, wiping her sneakers off at the door. "I'm not in a hurry."

After sweeping the loose hair off the floor, I grab the rolling cart with the curlers from where I had them plugged in at the back of the room, and invite her to have a seat at my station.

"Did you hear the news?" she asks, her eyes sparkling with mischief.

Mrs. Willowby comes in each week for a style, but I think it's mostly to gossip. She's been lonely since Mr. Willowby passed away. "No, what's new?"

I drape the cape around her neck, and get started setting her hair in the curlers.

"The city council is thinking of raising funds to open a community center. There's talk about adding a bake-off to the Christmas Fair this year, and a bachelor auction near Valentine's Day." Her eyebrows bounce up and down. "That one was my idea."

"Why, Mrs. Willowby, I didn't know you were looking," I tease. She may be in her eighties, but that doesn't mean she has to stay single. Though, what will it say about me if Mrs. Willowby gets a boyfriend before I do?

"Oh, no, dear." She giggles. "I'm much too old. Besides, I've already had the great love of my life, God rest his soul."

A community center would be a great idea. Right now, the only place to host a gathering is the church, and that's usually booked.

Once her hair's in curlers, I set her up under the dryer and set the timer. Moving back to the front counter, I finish folding the towels and put them in the cabinet between stations before returning the basket to the back room.

The alarm sounds, letting me know it's time to finish styling Mrs. Willowby's hair. Walking over to the row of driers, I lift the top and help her to her feet. "Any big plans today?"

She smiles, her red stained lips tugging up at the corners. "I'm meeting with some volunteers to go over these fundraising ideas." She rubs her hands together gleefully. "I volunteered to help organize the bachelor auction since no one else wanted to do it."

I can't contain the bubble of laughter that escapes me. "You're something else."

She winks. "That's what my Don used to say, too. He loved all of me."

I help her into the chair, and pull the curlers gently from her graying locks. I hope I am as animated as she is when I'm older. Right now, it feels like all I do is work and worry about the business. My aunt had established a solid clientele, but when she left, many of the older women worried I wouldn't do as good a job. It's taken me some time to prove myself.

Which has made business slower than I'd hoped, pushing back the upgrades I want to do, and obliterating my dating life.

"When are you going to get yourself a new sign?" Gabby asks, stepping through the door just as Mrs. Willowby's putting her overcoat back on. "Hi, Mrs. W. How are you today?"

"I'm great, dear. It's really too bad that Heath isn't available anymore." She shakes her head. "He'd bring in the big bucks. A soldier, and a mama's boy . . . doesn't get much better than that. I guess I'll just have to ask Hudson to help."

Gabby looks at me, her eyebrows stitched together in confusion. "I'm sorry. What?"

"Anne will fill you in. Won't you, dear? I really must run. I'd like to go to the Coffee Loft before my meeting. See and be seen, you know." She fluffs her hair. "Thanks, dear. Wonderful job, as usual." She gives a little wave and steps out the front door into the cold.

"What on earth was that about?" Gabby asks. "Is she trying to sell Heath?"

She follows me back to my chair while I attempt to explain. "I think she's more excited about a bachelor auction than she is about getting a community center going," I say, once I've filled her in.

Gabby laughs and nods her head. "I think you're probably right."

"So, what brings you by? You're not on the schedule for a few more weeks, right?" I take my time sanitizing the curlers and cleaning up my station.

"Nope. I stopped in to see if you wanted to come over for dinner. Heath's going out with the guys tonight and I don't feel like eating alone. Ever since we got engaged, we've tried to eat together every night when I'm not at work. It feels strange to eat alone now."

"I can't tonight. I've got the holiday dinner for the volunteers at the nursing home." My stomach growls, reminding me I didn't eat breakfast. I open the drawer at my station and pull out a fruit bar, open it, and take a big bite.

"Oh, man. I was really hoping you'd be able to come. I was planning on making some chili."

My feet ache already, and today's going to be another long day, but I already committed to the dinner. "Oh, darn, I'm sorry. Another time. I do love chili."

She grins. "I know. That's why I was making it. Plus, it reheats well and is great when it's this cold outside."

"You could always see if Mrs. Atkins would like company for dinner."

She grins. "I'm having lunch with her this afternoon. I'll ask her." She glances at her watch. "That reminds me. I should go. I've got some errands to run before I meet up with her."

She wraps me in a hug. "See ya. Have fun tonight. Oh, and if Shawn asks you out again, you should say yes."

I laugh. "Get out of here."

She blows me a kiss on her way out the door. "I just want to see you happy," she calls out as the door closes.

I *am* happy. Mostly.

CHAPTER TWO

Hudson

"LOOKING GOOD," BRADLEY SAYS when I make it to work a few minutes late. "Did you get your haircut?"

I run my hand over my head. I hate getting my hair done. It always feels so weird when it's freshly cut. "Yeah. Sorry I'm late."

Bradley pops the rest of the donut he's eating into his mouth and smiles. "No worries, man." He licks his fingers and wipes his hands on his jeans. "You can be a few minutes late. This time." He points at me and heads to his makeshift office.

I make myself a cup of coffee and head to the back, where I hear Heath busy at work already. "Hey, sorry I'm late." My tool belt clangs as I wrap it around my waist and buckle it.

"You get a haircut?" Heath asks when he turns around and sees me.

Jeez. Why is everyone commenting on my hair? It wasn't that long, was it? "Yeah. I stopped into Masters Cuts and More this morning on my way to work." I grab a pair of safety glasses and put them on.

Heath stares at me for thirty seconds before breaking out into a grin and slapping me on the shoulder. "You went to see Anne?"

I shake my head. "No, I went to get a haircut. Just so happens, Anne runs the only salon in town." I look away. "Are we going to get to work, or stand around gossiping?"

I don't want to get into this right now. I'm the fun guy. The guy who's never going to settle down. Nope. No thanks. I don't want to put in all that effort and end up alone, anyway. Sure, it works out for some people, but there are no guarantees. My dad's living proof of that. He fell in love, got married, and got saddled with me when Mom decided she didn't want the domestic life after all. Not that he'd ever complained, but I can't imagine taking on all that responsibility. Nah, I'm good.

"I'm not the one who was late. Slacker." Heath points a hammer at me before turning and getting back to the task he was busy with.

I grab a nail gun and get to work. We're hanging the drywall that will separate the smaller exam rooms from the surgical area in the back. "I'm glad we're finally getting a vet's office in town," I say when we take a break. "I'm getting tired of taking Purcasso over to Lost Creek for his annual visits and nail trims."

Heath laughs. "Purcasso? You named your cat Purcasso?"

I shrug. "He was missing an ear when I adopted him."

"You know that's the wrong artist, right?" Heath asks.

"Yeah, I know. But 'Purr Gogh' didn't have the same ring to it." I shrug my shoulders.

Heath laughs and shakes his head. "Didn't picture you as a cat guy. Though I didn't picture you as an art history buff, either."

I wag my eyebrows up and down. "You don't know me as well as you think you do. Besides, dogs need more attention than cats."

He nods. "You're right. Maybe Gabby would like a cat."

"Dude," I say, shaking my head. "Maybe don't buy her a pet until after you're married and can be there to help her with it. And you should clear it with her first."

He grins. "Good thinking."

The next few hours pass quickly as we work together to hang the drywall and tape it off.

"Want to head over to Beats and Eats for lunch?" Heath asks, setting his tool belt on the table near the front doors. "I'm starving and I brought nothing to eat."

The thought of eating the sandwich and chips I'd tossed into my lunchbox this morning doesn't seem appealing. "Sure, but you're driving."

He laughs and digs his keys out of his pocket. "Hey, boss, we're getting lunch. Want to come?"

Bradley shakes his head. "No thanks. I've got some errands to run. I'll grab something while I'm out."

"All right," I say, rubbing my stomach. "But don't say we didn't invite you."

He laughs. "Go on. I'll see you this afternoon."

Heath and I walk across the street and climb into his truck. He pulls out and heads toward Beats and Eats. The best diner in town. Though, why Ms. Daisy didn't call it Daisy's Diner is beyond me. Seems like a missed opportunity, honestly.

Once we are inside and seated, I look around for Gabby. "Is Gabby not working today?"

Heath grins. "I don't come here just to see her, you know."

I laugh. "Sure you don't."

"She's off. She mentioned having lunch with my mom today." Heath's smile lights up his entire face.

I'm not jealous. Not at all. I know Heath hasn't had it easy either. His dad took off when he was a kid, leaving him to care for his mom who got cancer when he was away serving in the Army, and I watched him and Gabby struggle to find their way back together.

That's heavy.

Too heavy.

Which is why I'm avoiding relationships . . . even if Anne is the sweetest woman I've ever met and has occupied my waking thoughts for months now, plus a few of my dreams.

"So, you like her?" Heath asks, flipping his menu over and scanning the lunch options.

"Who?" There's no way he can read minds, and I know my forehead's not a scrolling billboard displaying my thoughts . . . right? I rub my hand across my forehead. Nothing. Good.

"Anne." He looks up and folds his hands together on the table in front of him.

Raising an eyebrow, I give a small shake of my head. "You know better than that. I just think she's friendly, that's all. Besides, she's friends with Gabby, so I'm sure we'll be around each other a lot more once you two are married. I'm just being nice." I can't want more from her. Even if I haven't gotten her laugh out of my head since Heath's birthday in August.

"Uh-huh. Keep telling yourself that, then."

"Just order your food," I say, as Patty walks up to the table, her notepad in hand.

"Hey, guys." She smiles. "What can I get you today?"

"The usual," Heath says, passing back the menu. "And a Coke, please."

"You got it." Patty slides his menu behind her pad and turns to me. "And for you?"

I glance back at the menu. "I'll take the cheeseburger plate, please. And a chocolate shake, if it's not too much trouble."

She smiles. "Coming right up." She takes my menu and slides it behind Heath's before turning and heading to the computer on the back counter.

"She's pretty," I say. "Maybe I should ask her out." The words feel slimy in my mouth. She is pretty, but I don't feel the slightest bit of attraction to her. It's not just her, though. I haven't been attracted to anyone else since meeting Anne.

Heath laughs and slaps his hand on his leg. "That's the best face I've ever seen you pull. Looks like you just ate a lemon and kissed a frog at the same time."

"What?" I ask. "I'm just saying. She's single. I'm single. Maybe she'd be up for dinner. Nobody enjoys being dateless during the holidays." I fight to keep my face passive. A few months ago, I would've asked her out without a second thought.

"Seriously, how many dates have you been on since my birthday? I haven't been hearing nearly as much about your love life these days." Heath looks at me, a knowing smirk on his mug.

"I've been on dates," I say, looking around the diner. "I just don't feel like talking about them all." Truth be told, I've been on one date. And it was a disaster. I spent the entire dinner comparing her to Anne. By the time I paid our check, she had her keys out and was ready to leave. She never returned my calls after that, either.

I don't blame her. I wasn't my normal suave self.

"Here we are," Patty says, setting our drinks on the table. "Your food's coming right up. Sorry for the delay. We're busy this afternoon."

"No worries," Heath says. "Take your time."

She smiles and walks back to the counter to grab our plates from the warming window. She places them both on a tray and heads straight back to us. "Here you go."

The smell of beef and fried potatoes fills my nose, and my stomach growls loudly. "Thanks," I say, grabbing a fry and popping it into my mouth only to realize it's way too hot and I've just burned the inside of my mouth.

"Careful," she says, eyeing me. "It's hot."

I nod, tears in my eyes. "Got it," I croak out once I've finally swallowed the lava-hot fry.

Heath laughs again, and I swear if he weren't my friend, I'd want to smack him in the head. He and I haven't worked together long, but we've become fast friends. When he joined the crew, I was already pulling away from the guys I hung out with in college. Most of them are getting married and having babies. I'm happy for them, but that's not where I'm at in my life.

Heath was single when he started. Or so I thought. Turns out, he had his heart set on his first love.

We spend the next few minutes eating our lunch in comfortable silence, and I'm grateful for a break from the interrogation about my love life. Or lack thereof. It's not that I don't enjoy spending time with a woman. I do. I just don't see the point in handing my heart to someone for them to break. So, I try to make it clear that I'm not looking for forever. Just someone to spend time with. More like friends, really. That seems to go over like a ton of bricks.

Heath's phone buzzes in his pocket. He takes it out and reads the incoming message. Typing something back, he grins and tucks it away again.

"A message from Gabby?"

He nods. "Yep. Let's get back to work."

After paying our bills, Heath drives us back to the job site and parks his truck. "I really like what Austin Davis is doing with this old bank building," Heath says.

I nod. "Me too. It's definitely going to be unique." Usually when people hire us to renovate a space, they want everything removed and to start fresh. This guy, a veterinarian, wants to keep some features from the old building. Meshing the old with the new.

"You're not wrong about that." Heath heads inside, and I follow closely behind him, stomping the last bits of slush off my boots at the door.

We busy ourselves mixing and applying the first coat of joint compound on the seams. I'm lost in thought, replaying my conversation with Anne this morning, when Heath taps me on the shoulder.

"Time to go," Heath says, holding up his phone. "I'll see you at McFadden's?"

I nod. "I'll be there." A guys' night is just what I need to get my mind off of a certain gorgeous woman with sparkling green eyes.

CHAPTER THREE

Anne

BY THE TIME I close up shop, run home to change my clothes and feed Shelby, I'm late getting to McFadden's for the monthly volunteer meetup. I park my little VW Bug in the only open space I can find, and hop out.

My shoes crunch on the gravel as I rush to the front doors. I texted Shawn that I was running late and to order my usual. Hopefully, he did. I'm starving. Pulling open the heavy wooden doors, I pause and look around, letting my eyes adjust to the dimmer lighting. Shawn waves his hand in the air and points at an open seat next to him.

I nod and make my way through the tables to the group of men and women who make up the volunteer team for Lost Creek Assisted Living. "Hey, guys," I say, hanging my purse on the seat Shawn saved, and plopping down. "Sorry I'm late."

A chorus of "No problem," and "Glad you could make it" greets me. "Did you order for me?" I ask Shawn quietly.

He nods. "I got you a Diet Coke, and a cheeseburger smothered in A1, with fries and a side of ranch, just like you always get." He grins and leans in closer. "When are you going to let me take you out and really wine and dine you?"

Heat fills my cheeks. "Shawn," I say reproachfully, "you know we're just friends." Truth be told, he is a good guy, but I'm just not into him. I can't seem to keep my thoughts away from a certain construction worker. Even though that's the last place they should be wandering.

"Can't blame a guy for trying," he says before turning his attention to Molly.

Shawn and I started on the volunteer team around the same time. He's a relentless flirt, but that's what makes him popular amongst the older women at the nursing home. Thankfully, he's a good sport about being turned down, otherwise, things would be awkward.

The server arrives and passes out everyone's drinks while Beckett, the volunteer coordinator, is gathering everyone's attention. "Thank you all for coming out to the annual Volunteer Holiday Dinner. I am sure I don't need to tell you that your time and service mean the world to the residents." He looks at each of us. "With Christmas coming, I'm happy to announce Piney Brook Christian Church is donating little crocheted gifts for all the residents." The six volunteers around the table, including myself, clap. "However, we still need two people who wouldn't mind helping serve meals on Christmas Eve."

Beckett looks around. My hand itches to go up, but that's the night my family celebrates. Thankfully, Shawn raises his hand, as does Molly.

"Perfect. Thank you." He writes something on the notepad in front of him. "If there's nothing else pressing," he says, nodding toward the kitchen. "I think we can just enjoy the meal tonight."

The low murmur of conversation picks up, and I take a minute to look around the packed dining room. McFadden's is usually busy on the nights we come, but tonight seems busier than usual. My attention's pulled back to the table when Shawn reaches over and squeezes my shoulder.

"I'm sorry," I say, shaking my head. "I zoned out. What was that?"

Shawn nods his head toward a booth in the back. "Don't look now, but someone's been staring daggers at me since you came in."

"What?" I ask, confused. "Why?"

Shawn shrugs his shoulders. "You tell me. Here he comes."

"Anne," Hudson says as he approaches the table. "I'm surprised to see you here." He eyes Shawn warily.

I push up from my seat and give him a side hug. "Hey, Hudson. Fancy running into you tonight." I gesture around the table. "These are my friends, Beckett, Molly, Abe, Heather, Christina, and Shawn. Everyone, this is Hudson. We're having our monthly volunteer meeting for the Lost Creek Nursing Home."

"Nice to meet you all," Hudson says, smiling his big goofy grin that I want to keep all for myself. Wait . . . What? No, that's crazy. I watch the way Molly's posture shifts, leaning in just slightly, and I can't blame her. Hudson has that effect on people. Well, not me. Or at least . . . I try to remain immune to his charm.

"You volunteer at Lost Creek?" he asks, and it takes me a moment to realize he's directing the question at me.

"Every month," I say, hoping my voice sounds steadier than it feels. "Haircuts, mostly. Some of the residents can't get out much, so I bring the salon to them."

His face softens. "That's really nice, Anne."

The way he says my name sends a flutter through my chest. It's just two syllables. It shouldn't affect me like this.

"It's not a big deal," I say, shrugging.

"It is, though." He holds my gaze a beat longer than necessary. "I'm having dinner with Heath and a few of the guys." He motions over his shoulder. I look in that direction and wave at Heath who's staring over at us, an odd expression on his face. "It looks like your food's here, so I'll let you eat. Nice seeing you." He leans in and gives me another hug, holding me a bit too long. "Have a good night."

"Thanks. You, too." I watch as he gives a last wave to the table and heads back to his friends.

"So," Shawn says, drawing the word out. "He's handsome." He nudges me with his elbow. "Is that why you're turning me down?"

I drop my head, trying to hide the blush I know is forming on my cheeks. "He's a friend of a friend, really. He's definitely handsome, but he's also not interested."

"You sure about that?" Shawn asks. "He's still sneaking glances at you as we speak."

I fight the urge to turn my head and peek. "He's just a big ole flirt, kind of like someone else I know." I pick up my burger and take a huge bite, groaning when the sharpness of the cheddar and the tang of the A1 Sauce touch my tongue.

"Who eats a burger with A1 Sauce?" Molly asks, shuddering. "Why not ketchup or mayo like normal?"

I laugh and finish my bite. "I don't know. It's how Dad always made my burgers."

"You know that's her regular order," Abe says. "Weird as it may be." That earns a few chuckles from the table.

"Don't knock it until you try it," I say, before popping a ranch covered french fry into my mouth. At that, everyone laughs and goes back to their side conversations.

The noise of the restaurant wraps around me—silverware clinking, someone laughing too loud by the bar, a country song playing low through the speakers. McFadden's always smells like woodsmoke and fried onions, and tonight is no different. The Christmas lights strung along the rafters cast everything in a warm glow.

I should be focused on my friends. On the conversation Heather's having about her grandkids. Or the way Abe keeps stealing fries off Christina's plate when she's not looking.

But my thoughts keep drifting to the booth in the back corner.

Stop it, I tell myself. *He's just being friendly. That's all it is.*

Except friendly doesn't explain the way my pulse kicked up when he hugged me. Or the way his hand lingered on my shoulder a moment too long. Or the way he looked at Shawn like he wanted to set him on fire.

My skin prickles and I can't resist glancing toward Hudson's table. Sure enough, his eyes are on me, a half smirk on his lips. He's so handsome, it's ridiculous. Just then, he motions toward his lip with his fingers and winks. I stick out my tongue, and sure enough, a drip of ranch is sliding down my chin. I grab a napkin and wipe my face. If the floor could open up and swallow me now, that'd be great.

When everyone's about finished eating, I stand and grab my purse. "I'm heading out," I say, slipping the strap over my head. "Thanks for dinner."

"You're welcome," Beckett says. "See you next week."

I nod. "I'll be there." Each month, I spend a Saturday morning at the nursing home giving free haircuts to the residents. It's a small thing I can do, but it means a lot to them. Especially the men and women who aren't able to get out as much.

"Give me a call if you change your mind," Shawn says, standing and pulling me into a quick hug. "I'd love to take you out sometime."

"You got it," I say.

Just as I reach the front door, I feel a hand on my elbow. I turn and look right into Hudson's deep brown eyes.

"I'll walk you out," he says, pushing the door open. Then he leads me through with his hand on the small of my back.

"Um, thanks," I squeak out. The zing of awareness, which is racing up my spine from where his hand is touching me, makes me feel off balance.

Why couldn't I feel that zing with Shawn? He's made it clear he's interested. He's about my same age. We have a lot in common, but . . . there's nothing there.

"Anytime," he says, offering me that goofy grin. "Why isn't your boyfriend walking you out?"

"My boyfriend?" I ask, confusion clear in my tone. "What boyfriend?"

He tips his head back to the restaurant. "The guy who couldn't keep his hands off you." He raises an eyebrow and pins those dark chocolate eyes on mine.

"Shawn's just a friend, like I said." Is he jealous? Of course not. That would be silly.

Hudson's jaw tightens almost imperceptibly. "He doesn't act like just a friend."

"Well, he is." I cross my arms, suddenly aware of the chill in the air. December in Piney Brook doesn't mess around. "Not that it's any of your business."

"You're right." He shoves his hands in his jacket pockets. "It's not."

Does he want it to be?

We stand there for a moment, the silence stretching between us. A truck rumbles past on the main road, headlights sweeping across the gravel lot. Somewhere inside, I can hear muffled laughter.

"Why did you come out here?" I ask quietly.

He doesn't answer right away. Just looks at me with those impossibly dark eyes, like he's weighing something. "Wanted to make sure you got to your car okay."

"It's twenty feet from the door."

"Thirty, at least." The corner of his mouth twitches. "I counted."

I bite back a smile. "That's very thorough of you."

"I'm a thorough guy."

The gravel crunches under his boots as he shifts his weight, and somehow, he's closer now. Close enough that I catch the faint scent of his cologne—it's warm and woodsy and makes me want to lean in.

Don't, I warn myself. *This is a bad idea.*

I take a step back, willing myself to get it together. Heath is a friend. He's not interested in a relationship at all, let alone with me. It would be stupid to develop *those* kinds of feelings. But my heart isn't listening. Great.

As we approach my car, Hudson drops his hand from my back, and I feel the loss of his touch acutely. He stands back and gives me room to open the door. When I turn back around, it seems he's moved closer to me. My eyes drop to his full lips. I wonder what it would be like to kiss him.

I glance back up to his eyes, wishing I could read his mind.

"Well," he says, clearing his throat and draping his arm over the car door. "Drive safe."

I suck in a breath and nod. "Thanks." I slip into the car and smile. "You as well." He closes the door, and I put my seat belt on before starting the car and glancing back in his direction. He's standing off to the side, watching me. I back out of the parking space and glance in the rearview mirror as I drive off. He's still there, his eyes on my car as I pull away.

I never imagined Hudson being chivalrous. And why does the thought of him being jealous send my heart into overdrive? *Surely I'm imagining things.*

Right?

CHAPTER FOUR

Hudson

"YOU GOOD?" HEATH ASKS, when I slide back into the booth.

"Yep." I pick up my drink and finish it in one long gulp. "I think I'm calling it a night."

Heath laughs. "Man, we've only stayed this long because you seemed to be preoccupied." He raises his eyebrows in question. "So, what's going on there?"

I shake my head and throw a twenty on the table. "Nothing."

Tim, the head of the north Cobb County crew, laughs. "If that's nothing, I'd hate to see how you are when it's something. You were practically growling at that guy."

I turn my head toward the man in question. He's walking another woman—Molly, I think her name was—to the door. Figures he'd flirt with Anne all night and not even have the decency to walk her out. "I was not."

That's a lame response. I was and we all know it.

Heath snorts into his drink. "Sure you weren't. You just happened to be white-knuckling your glass every time he touched her shoulder."

I glance down at my hands. He's not wrong. There's still tension coiled in my grip.

"She's a grown woman," I mutter. "She can talk to whoever she wants."

"Uh-huh." Tim exchanges a look with Beau. "That's exactly what a guy says when he doesn't care at all."

I ignore them both and steal another glance toward Anne's table. She's laughing at something Molly said, her head tipped back, the dim light catching the gold in her hair. Something in my chest tightens.

I watched her all through dinner. Couldn't help it. The way she scrunched her nose when she took that first bite of her burger. The way she wiped ranch off her chin and stuck her tongue out at me like we were kids on a playground. The way that Shawn guy kept leaning into her space, finding excuses to touch her arm, her shoulder, her back.

It shouldn't bother me.

It does.

I drain the last of my water. "I walked her to her car."

That gets everyone's attention.

"Did you now?" Tim says, grinning. "And how'd that go?"

I think about the way she looked up at me in the parking lot, her green eyes catching the glow from the streetlights. The way my hand didn't want to leave the small of her back. The way I almost—*almost*—leaned in.

"Fine," I say. "It went fine."

Heath shakes his head. "You're hopeless."

"All right, then," Beau, a guy from Tim's team, says. "As fun as this has been, and it has been fun, I think I'm ready to call it a night, too."

After paying our tabs, we say our goodbyes in the parking lot.

"Hey, Hudson," Heath calls, stopping me just before I get into my truck. "Don't hurt her."

I shake my head. "Not an issue."

He stares at me for a minute. "Keep telling yourself that."

I watch as he walks to his truck, whistling a little tune as he goes. Just because he's in love and getting married doesn't mean I need to be.

A vision of Anne in a white wedding dress comes to mind and I shake it away. *I'm not meant to get married and have a family.* I remind myself. I decided that when I was fifteen years old. Nothing's changed.

Then why can't I stop picturing it with Anne?

I start the truck and sit there for a minute, letting the engine idle.

The thing is, I know exactly why I made that decision at fifteen. When my mom left and I had to watch my dad fall apart in the months that followed—drinking too much, working too little, forgetting to buy groceries or pay the electric bill. Love didn't save them. Marriage didn't keep her there.

So I decided I'd never put myself in that position. Never give someone the power to wreck me like that.

It's worked out fine so far. I've dated. Had fun. Kept things casual and walked away before anyone got too attached—including me.

But Anne ...

I grip the steering wheel and pull out of the parking lot.

Anne's different. I don't know how or why, but she's gotten past my defenses. Every time I see her, I want to know more. What makes her laugh. What keeps her up at night. Why she volunteers at a nursing home giving free haircuts to strangers.

She's kind in a way that seems effortless. Genuine.

And I have no business thinking about her like this.

I turn up the radio, hoping the noise will drown out my thoughts. It doesn't.

I pull at the tie around my neck, and wonder for the fifth time in fifteen minutes if I can ditch it. I pick up the invitation and sigh. Tonight's Heath and Gabby's engagement party. His mom clearly stated "semiformal" on the invitation.

The things I do for my friends.

I grab my keys and lock up the apartment before hopping in the truck and heading over to the church. Mrs. A rented the space again since it worked so well for his birthday party. I'm sure she's been there all day decorating and setting up. I smile. There's not much that woman wouldn't do for her son.

A pang of regret hits me square in the chest. Usually I don't even think about Mom being gone, but every once in a while, at things like this, I wonder why I wasn't enough for her to stick around.

I pull my truck into an empty parking space and hop out. The parking lot's nearly full of cars and people milling about. Spotting Olivia, Heath's friend from his time in the Army, and her family, I make my way over to them to say hi.

"Hi. Hudson, wasn't it?" Olivia says, shaking my hand. "Nice to see you again."

"You, too. Is the happy couple here yet?" I ask, looking around at the parked cars.

"Not yet. I think they'll be here any minute, though," Dominic, Olivia's husband, says.

Just then, Mrs. A steps outside and calls everyone in. "They're almost here. Time to make your way inside."

I stop when I reach her and place a kiss on her cheek. "You look radiant," I tell her.

She pats my shoulder. "Go flirt with someone your own age." Laughing, but then leans in closer to say, "but thank you."

I step inside the room and, sure enough, Mrs. A's outdone herself. Streamers in pale pink and white are strung across the ceiling. A huge sign is taped up along the back wall that says, "Soon to be Mr. and Mrs." Balloons are at every table, the pink and white orbs bobbing up and down with the air conditioning. Along the far wall, tables are set up with hors d'oeuvres and cupcakes.

I make my way to a back table and smile. Anne is standing, her back to me, talking with Reese, one of her and Gabby's friends. Anne's caramel-color hair cascades down her back in waves. She turns and her eyes meet mine. For a moment, it feels like I can't breathe. She's stunning. The soft green of the wrap dress hugs her curves in all the right spots. It's like it was made for her.

"You look breathtaking," I say when I finally reach her side. "So do you, Reese." I can't peel my eyes away from Anne.

"Sure," Reese says. "What color am I wearing?" she asks, laughing when I don't answer right away.

I turn and take in her outfit. A pretty red-and-white-striped jumpsuit. "Was that a trick question?"

She shakes her head and goes to comment, but gets interrupted when the man and woman of the hour make their grand entrance.

After everyone has said hello to the couple, we settle into our assigned seats. I'm pleasantly surprised when I discover Anne is seated next to me. It's only because she's witty and fun to be around. Not because I have feelings for her.

Heath's words from the other night echo in my head. *Keep telling yourself that.*

"So," Anne says, once we've gotten our plates and are seated again. "How are things?"

I finish chewing my bite of bruschetta. "Good. Just working, really. You?"

She smiles, and the room disappears. "Same."

I blink my eyes. Hard. Get it together, Hudson.

I reach for my drink just to have something to do with my hands. "You look really nice tonight," I say, then immediately want to kick myself. I already told her she looked breathtaking. Now I sound like a broken record.

But she just ducks her head, a small smile playing at her lips. "Thanks. You clean up pretty well yourself." She gestures at my tie. "I don't think I've ever seen you in anything other than work boots and sawdust."

"The sawdust is my signature look."

"It suits you." She takes a sip of her drink, and I watch the way her throat moves when she swallows.

Stop staring.

"So," I say, scrambling for something to keep the conversation going. "How do you know Heath and Gabby? I know you and Gabby are friends, but I never got the full story."

Her face lights up. "We met at a book club a few years back. Gabby wandered in looking for a romance novel recommendation, and I steered her toward one of my favorites. We've been friends ever since."

"Let me guess. You recommended something romantic."

She laughs, and the sound hits me right in the chest. "Maybe. What's wrong with romance?"

"Nothing at all." I lean back in my chair, enjoying the pink creeping up her cheeks. "I'm just trying to picture Gabby reading that."

"She loved it, for the record."

"I don't doubt it."

"So, how do you know Shawn?" I ask. Smooth idiot. "You know what? Never mind. That wasn't what I meant to ask. I meant to ask, how was your dinner the other night?"

There, that's better. What was I thinking asking her about that guy again?

She blushes, and it's the cutest thing I've ever seen.

"He's a friend. The dinner was nice. It's good to get out sometimes, you know. Mingle. I like living by myself, but sometimes it gets lonely."

I think about my empty apartment waiting for me. "Yeah, I know what you mean." I hadn't ever considered being on my own as being lonely, but now that she's said it, I guess she's right.

She laughs and shakes her head. "I doubt someone as handsome as you spends much time feeling lonely." She slaps her hand over her mouth. "Sorry. I just mean, I'm sure there are a ton of women waiting to spend time with you." Her cheeks turn cherry red, and she looks like she wishes she could melt away.

"How sweet. You think I'm handsome?" I ask. Could she be attracted to me, too?

She rolls her eyes. "I'm not blind. Everyone thinks you're attractive."

I lift my arms and pose like I'm in a bodybuilding competition. "Oh, really?" I should let her off the hook. Change the subject. Make a joke.

Instead, I lean in a little closer. "What if I told you I'm not interested in tons of women?"

Her breath catches. Just barely, but I notice.

"I'd say that's hard to believe," she manages.

"Why?"

She gestures vaguely at me—my face, my shoulders, all of me. "Because ... look at you."

"I'm looking at you," I say, and my voice comes out lower than I intended.

For a second, neither of us moves. The noise of the party fades to a distant hum. It's just her eyes on mine, wide and uncertain and—hopeful?

Then I hear Mrs. Atkins approaching and lean back, breaking the spell.

"Of course, dear," Mrs. Atkins says, patting my shoulder as she walks by. "And so humble, too."

Anne and Patty burst out laughing.

"Hey," I complain. "I'm humble." At that, both women double over, laughing even harder. As I watch Anne laugh, tingles spread up the nape of my neck, and I realize I have on a goofy smile. I can't look away.

When did I start finding someone's laugh attractive?

Probably about the time Anne decided to crawl under my skin.

The question now is, what am I going to do about it?

CHAPTER FIVE

Anne

WALKING DOWN THE STREETS of Piney Brook in December feels so magical. It's my first day off in what feels like weeks, and I'm excited to soak up some Christmas spirit.

Christmas decorations are in every window, and the town square is filled with people milling about, enjoying the giant lit tree in the center of the lawn. I pass by the flower shop and wave at Joy, the owner, who's busy redoing the flower displays in her window.

I turn the corner and stop outside the Coffee Loft. The smell of freshly brewed coffee and sugar is too much to pass up, so I step inside and get in line. The moms who've been in the salon weren't joking when they said business was booming. Nearly every table is filled with people enjoying their midday pick me up. Through the glass pane of the connecting door, I see Lacey checking in a family. They've really made their dreams come true, these two.

I smile to myself. It's good to see small businesses thrive. Especially in a small town. I always dreamed of living in the big city after school. I imagined doing hair for celebrities.

After graduation, though, all I wanted was to come back home and live a simple life. I had a taste of the big city at school, and I can confidently say it's not for me.

The line moves forward, and I step forward with it, using the time to look around. Christmas music plays softly through the overhead speakers. Stuffed snow families adorn the counters and tabletops. Potted poinsettias bring a cheery color to the bustling dining room. It's festive without being over the top.

A tap at my shoulder has me turning around. "Hudson! Hey, what are you doing here?" Those deep brown eyes sparkle with amusement. Besides the day at the salon, I don't think I've ever seen him look anything but joyful.

"I'm out doing some Christmas shopping," he says before cracking up and shaking his head. "No, I'm not. I was just over at Brant's automotive getting an oil change and stopped in for some coffee and cookies on my way home."

I burst out laughing. "You almost had me!" We shuffle forward when the line moves. "Unlike you, I *am* out shopping this afternoon."

He grins. "Can I buy your coffee?"

I tilt my head and study him. "Sure. Thanks."

"What can I get you today?" Aurora asks when it's our turn to order.

"I'll have a s'mores hot chocolate and a French cruller, please." I step back a bit, allowing room for Hudson to move closer to the counter. He places his order, a hot coffee with cream and extra sugar and half a dozen cookies, and taps his card to pay.

"Looks like you've been busy," I say to Aurora as she busies herself making our drinks.

"We have! I've had to hire extra help. It's been the most profitable December since I've been in business." She slides my mug across the counter and plates a danish for me. "Here you are."

"Why don't you get us a table while I wait on my coffee?" Hudson asks.

"Oh, sure." I turn and scan the room, looking for an empty space. Finding one over by the window, I carefully make my way through the crowded room and sigh in relief when I set the steaming mug on the waiting table top.

"Perfect," Hudson says, joining me and setting his cup and bag of treats on the table. "I hope you don't mind a bit of company."

I shake my head. "Not at all." Slipping my coat off, I hang it on the chair back and take a seat. "Cocoa's always better when you're with a friend."

He takes a sip of his coffee and smiles at me over the rim. "I like that."

After a moment of quiet, I ask, "What are your plans for the holidays?"

"Oh, the usual. Dad and I will deep fry a turkey and watch football and *Die Hard*." He takes a cookie out of the bag and snaps it in half. "Want to try it?"

I point to my donut and shake my head. "No thanks. *Die Hard*, huh? So, you're saying you like Christmas movies?" I chuckle at myself.

He throws his head back and a burst of laughter fills the air. "Finally! A woman who understands." He winks at me, and I feel myself blushing.

"I don't know what women you've been hanging out with, but if they don't think Die Hard is a Christmas movie, how do they explain the holiday party?" I shake my head. "Sad."

He studies me, a lopsided grin on his face. "You're right," he finally says. "Sad. So, what about you? Any big plans?"

I finish my sip of cocoa and smile. "Tonight, the girls and I are getting together for our annual movie marathon. No *Die Hard*, though. Unfortunately, I'm the only one who sees the festive vibe in that one."

Hudson smiles and picks up a napkin. Leaning forward, he wipes it across my nose. "You had a little cream," he says, settling back in his chair, calm as can be. Meanwhile, my heart's beating faster than a hummingbird's wings at a feeder in the summer.

"Thanks," I say, my voice breathless to my own ears.

"So, no action movies in the lineup for the night. Got it." He smiles and takes another bite of his cookie. The chocolate chunks poking out of the cookie make me wish I'd chosen that instead of the cruller.

"Nope."

He nods. "What do you do for Christmas?"

I wrap my hands around the warm mug. "Christmas Eve, I go to my parents' house. We go to church together, and then back to their house for dinner and presents. My dad's a paramedic and he always works on Christmas Day."

Hudson brushes crumbs off the front of his sweater. "That sounds like a nice time. What do you do on Christmas Day, then?"

"Usually, I watch Christmas movies, heat some leftovers and just relax." I observe his reaction. Most people think that's sad, but I'm used to it. It's how my family has done Christmas since I was a kid. Plus, I don't watch Christmas movies alone. I volunteer at the nursing home in town and we always watch at least one in the afternoon.

"Sounds nice."

I'm relieved when I realize he isn't pitying me. "It really is." I finish the last bite of my turnover and wipe my fingers on my napkin. "Thanks for the hot chocolate and the conversation."

"Thank you. Let me clean up our mess and I'll walk you out." He stacks the mugs and grabs the plate before heading to the corner of the room and placing them in the waiting dish bin.

"Ready?" he asks, grabbing his bag of remaining cookies from the table.

I stand and put my arms back through my coat sleeves. "Ready."

We say goodbye on the sidewalk, and I watch as he climbs in his truck and drives away. Seems there's more to Hudson than the flirtatious jokester everyone thinks he is. When he spoke about his dad, his eyes held so much compassion. For the first time, I wonder just how much he hides with his flirty behavior.

I park my car behind Lacey's SUV and carefully make my way up the driveway. I've got a platter of cheesecake-stuffed strawberries balanced on one hand, and a bottle of sparkling grape juice in the other.

"You're here," Reese says, opening the front door wide and stepping back. "Let me take something." She grabs the plate and bumps the door shut with her hip. "I'm so glad you could make it!"

I follow her through to the kitchen, where she sets the strawberries on the table with several other festively decorated items. "Looks like we have a delicious feast tonight."

She grins. "Everyone's in the family room. You can put your coat and bag in Elli's room. She's at Heather's this weekend."

"Thanks." After stowing my coat and purse, I head into the family room where Lacey's sitting cross-legged on the floor, telling a story about what sounds like an epic mess at A Children's Place.

"Hey guys," I say, when there's a pause in the story. "Good to see you all."

"Now the gang's all here," Morgan says, rubbing her small baby bump. "Can we please eat?"

"Come on," Reese says. "Let's feed her before she gets really cranky." Aurora, Lacey, Gabby, Morgan, Karlee, and I all follow her into the dining room.

"Pregnant ladies first," Morgan says, cackling. "Hey, it's got to be useful for something."

Reese laughs and motions for her to fill her plate. "You're too much. It's a good thing we love you."

Morgan pops a strawberry into her mouth and does a happy dance.

"What do you think the guys are up to?" Karlee asks.

"I'm not sure. I think they were going to watch football or something," Morgan says. She puts two more strawberries and some mini quiches on her plate and steps back from the table. "Brant's got the grill ready to go."

"It was nice of Daniel to let us have our party at his house," I say, snagging a plate and checking out the food options.

"I know," Reese says, blushing as red as her hair. "He's the best."

"When are you two getting married?" Gabby asks.

"Hey," I say, bumping my hip into Gabby. "Not everyone rushes to the altar."

Gabby blushes and shrugs. "We aren't rushing."

"I know. I'm just saying."

"Just wait," Karlee says. "When you find your person, you'll be just as anxious as Gabby is."

If I find my person. Lately, I'm thinking I'm destined to be alone.

Once everyone's stomachs are full. Reese cues up the first movie, and we settle in. Conversation ebbs and flows between scenes. When the first movie ends, Morgan's curled in a ball, fast asleep on the end of the couch.

"Guess she's tired," Lacey says softly, covering her with a blanket.

"I'm kind of tired myself," I say, standing to stretch. "I think I'm going to call it a night."

"Aww, but we were going to watch *Miracle on 34th Street.*" Reese pouts.

"We've seen it a hundred times. I think you'll be okay without me." I make my rounds, giving everyone, except the sleeping mama bear, a hug. "Thanks for a great night."

I step outside just in time to see Daniel getting out of his truck. A bouquet of red roses in his hand. "Wrapping up?" he asks.

"Yeah, I'm tired. I think the girls were planning to watch one more movie. You may want to hide out in your room, unless you like sad movies."

He salutes me. "Thanks for the tip. Drive safe."

What would it be like to have someone bring me flowers just because? I wonder if I'll ever find out.

Chapter Six

Hudson

Today's the Christmas Festival downtown. I debated not going, but then I heard about the Christmas bake-off and changed my mind. It's good to support your community, especially if it involves food.

I step out of the truck and into the bright sunshine. Thankfully, the roads are clear now that all the slush has melted off. This is the last weekend before Christmas, and people are out in droves. Lining sidewalks, stepping in and out of the shops that line Main Street, and huddled together beside booths where people are selling everything from jam to quilts.

The Christmas season is upon us.

I'm debating whether to leave my coat in the car and just wear my jeans and Arkansas sweatshirt when I spot a familiar face strolling by on the opposite sidewalk.

Forget the coat.

I shut the door, press the lock button on my keys before shoving them into my pocket, and hustle across the street. "Hey there, pretty lady."

Anne turns, her cheeks pink from the cool weather. "Hey, Hudson. Finally, out doing your Christmas shopping?"

I rock back on my heels. "Yep, and I came to check out the baked goods. I like to support the community, you know."

She giggles, and I wish I had a magic box to capture the sound in so I could listen to it repeatedly. "Of course. Couldn't be because you have a sweet tooth."

I shake my head. "Of course not. Those cookies were for Purcasso."

Her eyes widen comically. "Purcasso?"

"My cat," I say. "He's really got a problem. He can't stay away from the cookies."

She laughs, a full belly laugh. The kind where your eyes leak a little, and a ball of warmth unfurls in my chest. Maybe that's what it felt like when the Grinch's heart grew three sizes. Hmm.

"And to think, Shelby just likes the occasional scoop of tuna." She's still giggling when a woman who looks strikingly similar to her joins us. "Oh, Mom. This is Hudson, Heath's friend. Hudson, my Mom — Martha."

"Nice to meet you," I say, reaching for her hand and drawing it to my lips before placing a chaste kiss on the back of her hand. "I see where Anne gets her beauty." Martha blushes, and it makes her look so much like her daughter, I have to do a double take. "Well, I'll let you two enjoy your day. I was just stopping to say hello."

"It was lovely to meet you," Martha says, elbowing Anne in the side.

"See you later," Anne says, pinning her mom with a glare. "Enjoy your shopping."

"Oh, Hudson," Martha calls as I walk away. "Would you like to join us on Christmas Eve?"

"Mom!" Anne screeches. "You can't just go around inviting people to things like that."

I open my mouth to decline. "I'd love to." Wait, what?

Anne's mouth drops open as she looks from me to her mother. Martha claps her hands together gleefully. "Wonderful! Anne will get you the details."

"Mom, I don't even have his number." Anne frowns at her mother.

"Oh, well. No time like the present. The way you were talking about the gentleman, I was sure you already had his information."

Anne's entire face turns bright red. She'd give Rudolph's nose a run for its money. "You've been talking about me?" I ask. My cheeks hurt from smiling so big. The idea of Anne talking about me to her mother doesn't freak me out like it should. Nope, it makes me happy.

"I just mentioned you bought me coffee the other day. Aurora asked about you when we stopped in the Coffee Loft." She shrugs, clearly uncomfortable.

I take out my phone. "Why don't you enter your number into my contacts, and then I'll text you later?"

She hesitates, but moves to take the phone. After punching in her number, she passes it back. I hit dial and smile when I hear her phone ringing in her purse. "There. Now you have my number, too."

Her mother looks between us and smiles like the cat that just got the canary. "We'll see you in a few days," she says, taking Anne by the arm and guiding her to another table close by.

I watch as Anne gestures wildly while talking to her mother, who hasn't stopped smiling yet. What on earth did I just do?

"There you are, Hudson!" Mrs. Willowby appears from behind a booth of handmade quilts. Her eyes are sparkling with mischief and I glance around to see if there's anywhere I can hide. "Oh, no you don't," she says, wagging her finger. "I've been looking for you. I'm organizing the Valentine's Bachelor Auction for the new community center, and you, my dear boy, are the star of the show." She grins, her red lipstick smudged just a bit in the corners.

I can feel my neck get warm. I'm sure my ears are turning red, too. "I don't think I'm auction material, Mrs. W."

"Nonsense," she says, patting my arm. "A handsome young man like you with a soft spot for cats . . . you'll bring in the highest bid of the night. I'm sure of it." She winks at me. "Unless, of course, someone snatches you off the market before then."

I glance over my shoulder to where Anne and her mom were walking away. "Uhm," I say, trying to come up with a polite way to decline her crazy invitation.

She giggles. "Oh, I see." She gives me an exaggerated wink. "A certain someone caught your eye?"

"What? Oh, no. I was just . . ." What was I doing?

"Good, then I'll pencil you in. If anything changes, you just let me know." She pats my arm before shuffling away, probably to find her next victim. Err, bachelor.

Once I'm sure she's gone, I make my way through the tables, careful to go in the opposite direction of Mrs. Willowby.

Now, where's the bake-off?

I finally spot a tent with several tables of baked goods across the way. I stop at a table labeled Apple Blossom Ranch and grab a gift basket of jams and honey for my dad. Perfect. Christmas shopping is done. Unless . . . Should I bring something for Anne's parents? For Anne?

She did say they exchanged presents. Turning back around, I pick out another smaller basket for her parents. That leaves Anne. What do you get for the woman you can't stop thinking about?

I decide to take a closer look at some of the tables after I visit the bake goods table and put these baskets in the truck.

"Hudson," Ashlan says, when I approach the tent housing the sweet goodies. "Come to stock up for the holiday?"

I laugh. "You caught me." I glance around at the array of baked goods. Everything from cookies and brownies to cakes and cobblers line the tables. "What do you recommend?"

She points to the cobblers. "The apple cobbler from Apple Blossom Ranch is my favorite." She giggles. "I've sampled them all."

I nod. "Good advice. Thanks." After picking out several desserts, I stuff a hundred-dollar bill in the donation jar. She's occupied by a little boy with chocolate smeared on his face who looks like he can't wait to get his hands on another treat, so I skip telling Ashlan goodbye.

I hike back to the truck and carefully stow the purchases before making another pass at the tables. What on earth should I get Anne?

I straighten my tie in the mirror. I'd gone to the store and picked out an outfit special for today. Despite not going to church in years, I still know you should dress well. I just hope no one objects to my tie. I figured if I had to wear one, it would at least be funny.

Grabbing my keys and Anne's gift, which I put in a bag rather than show off my less than stellar wrapping skills, I head out to the truck. The gift basket for Anne's parents is already stowed safely inside.

I check the text she'd sent with the address and time, and run my finger around my collar. Getting into the truck, I punch the address into the GPS and hit drive. I'm meeting them at church and then following them to their house for dinner after. I still don't quite know how I ended up being invited, or why I agreed to go, but here I am, dressed in something other than jeans and work boots, with gifts nestled in the seat beside me.

I shake my head. *Who am I right now?*

I pull into the church parking lot and find a space at the back. Looks like half of Piney Brook is here this evening. I leave the gifts in the car and make my way to the front doors to meet Anne and her family.

The moment I spot Anne, the breath leaves my lungs. Her hair is curled in soft waves, flowing down her back. A red dress with longish sleeves hangs down to her calves.

She's breathtaking.

And glaring at me.

I hurry my steps. "You look beautiful," I say, when I finally reach her. "Merry Christmas."

"Is that a Santa cat?" she asks, pointing to my tie.

"What? I had to get it. He looks just like Purcasso."

She fights the grin that threatens to curve her ruby red lips. "Merry Christmas, Hudson." She shakes her head. "Come on. My parents are waiting for us."

I follow her inside to the pew where her parents are holding our seats. "Welcome," Martha says, standing and squeezing my hand. "I'm glad you could make it."

"Thank you. It's nice to see you again." Her dad stands, coming to his full height, which still leaves him about two inches shorter than me. "Mr. Masters," I say, reaching out to shake his hand. "A pleasure to meet you, sir."

"Nice to meet you." He sits back down and grabs the coats from the bench to make room for us to sit. "Have a seat. Service is about to start."

I sit and watch as the story of the Nativity is acted out. Laughing when the little kids forget their lines or knock something over. It's precious. And it's over before I know it.

Once her mother introduced me to just about everyone there, we file out of the church and onto the front patio. "Anne, you should ride with Hudson so he doesn't get lost."

Anne bites her lip, but doesn't argue. "Okay, you ready?"

Taking her hand, I slide it through my elbow and nod to her parents. "We'll be right behind you."

Her dad watches me warily. Like he's trying to figure out my end game. Me too, buddy. Me too.

I walk her to the truck and rearrange the presents so she can take the passenger seat. "Sorry about that," I say, stepping back and making room for her to climb up. "I wasn't expecting you to ride with me."

She gives me a look that says she wasn't either and steps up into the truck, settling herself in the passenger seat. Okay, then. I close her door carefully and make my way around the driver's side. Pulling up the address on my phone, I punch it into the GPS and hit drive. "I'm sorry."

Anne turns and faces me. "For what?"

"For invading your family time. I should have said no when your mom asked." I look away, waiting for traffic to ease up before I pull into the flow of cars trying to exit the church.

"Why didn't you?" she asks. Her voice is soft, almost a whisper.

"Honestly?" I ask, looking at her. "I don't know."

She stares at me blankly. "Okay, then."

"I opened my mouth, intending to say no, and found myself agreeing to come." I risk a glance in her direction. "I can't seem to say no where you're involved."

CHAPTER SEVEN

Anne

I TURN MY HEAD and look out the window. I'm not sure how to respond to that information. Thankfully, he's got the GPS. He doesn't need me to give him directions.

The heater in the truck is warm, and he's playing Christmas music softly. "I didn't peg you for a big Christmas person when we talked."

He chuckles. "I'm not. Not usually, anyway. There was never much reason to be."

Now I just feel like a wet blanket. "Oh. How come?"

Hudson clears his throat. "Well, I told you it's just me and Dad." He stops and shrugs.

"He didn't like Christmas?" I can't help but ask. I can't imagine my parents not making a big deal out of Christmas. They'd always insisted on all the holiday things. Even after I grew up and moved out.

"It's complicated," he says, carefully taking the turn down my parents' road.

"You don't have to tell me." I glance back out the window, taking in the lights that are just coming to life on the houses.

"My mom left at Christmas time." He says it so quietly I almost wonder if I imagined it. "The holidays were never the same after that."

"Oh, Hudson. I'm so sorry. That must have been hard." Tears fill my eyes, and I feel them wet my lashes.

"It was a long time ago," he says, reaching into his glove box and handing me a napkin. "No need to cry."

I nod. I'm quiet as he pulls into the driveway and parks. "I owe you an apology. I've been a bit rude about you joining us. I shouldn't have been. Christmas is a time to share joy, not snatch it."

He laughs. "Sweetheart, I don't think there's anything you could do that would snatch someone's joy. You're too pure."

I fight a smile. "You better stop saying things like that, or I might start thinking you like me." I chuckle at my silliness, except . . . I'm the only one laughing. Hudson's staring at me with an unreadable expression on his face. "Hudson? It was a joke, okay? I know you're not the guy who settles down."

He looks like I reached out and slapped his face. "I'm not? And you know this because?"

I shrug. "Gabby told me."

He nods. "Don't believe everything you hear," he says, before opening the door and stepping down from the truck.

Huh. What's that mean?

He helps me down from the truck, and grabs a gift basket and a bag from behind the seat. "You didn't have to bring anything," I say, pointing to the items.

"I know. I wanted to." He smiles and closes the truck door. "Lead the way."

We step into my parents' house, and it's like stepping into a Hallmark movie. The stairway is adorned with garland, the living room is dominated by a giant tree, and Christmas cards line the mantle.

"Wow," I hear Hudson mutter under his breath. "This is amazing."

"Thank you," Mom says, coming to take our coats. "Here, Ron, come take these things from Hudson and put them under the tree." She passes them to Dad, who quickly moves to do what she said. After hanging our coats, she points us toward the living room. "Dinner will be done in a few minutes. I just need to whip the potatoes."

"I can help, Mom," I say, stepping around her to get into the kitchen.

"Why don't you see if Hudson would like something to drink? Ron? You want a glass of sweet tea?"

"Please, dear," Dad says, already reaching for the remote.

"Do you want something to drink? We have water, tea, sparkling water. We may even have a bottle of wine somewhere."

Hudson smiles. "I'll have what he's having," he says, winking at me.

Something's different today, but I can't put my finger on it. He's the same ole flirt he's always been, but there's an undercurrent of something else. Maybe it's just holiday spirit. Who knows?

I step into the kitchen and make three glasses of sweet tea. Mom's already sipping sparkling water and adding butter to the potatoes. "Are you sure you don't need my help?"

She smiles and dips a spoon into the gravy. "I'm sure," she says, tasting the golden liquid and sighing. "All set in here."

I nod and carefully grab the drinks. "Okay, then."

When I get back to the living room, the game's on, and Dad and Hudson are discussing the rankings of the SEC teams, and how lumping the East and West divisions together this year affects each team's standings. A riveting conversation, I'm sure.

"Anne, did you know your boyfriend went to the University of Arkansas?" Dad asks cheerfully.

"My what? I ... what?" I ask, clearly confused. "Hudson's not ..." Before I can finish, Hudson stands and takes two of the glasses.

"I'm not officially her boyfriend," he says, handing Dad his glass. "She hasn't agreed to let me take her on an actual date yet."

Dad glances over at me and smiles. "She's always been a stubborn one."

I shake my head. "No. Hudson hasn't asked me on a date, yet," I say to defend myself. I hate when Dad calls me stubborn.

Hudson's face lights up brighter than the Christmas tree. "So, if I asked, you'd say yes?"

Dad chuckles. "Well played, son."

I feel my cheeks heat with embarrassment. "I don't know. Guess you'll have to ask and find out."

"Dinner's ready," Mom calls from the dining room.

Everyone shuffles in and takes a seat. Dad at the head of the table, Mom in her spot right beside him. I sit in my usual seat across from Mom, leaving Hudson to sit across from Dad at the open end of the table.

"Let's say grace," Dad says, bowing his head.

I sneak a peek at Hudson out of the corner of my eye. His hands are folded and his head is bowed like he does this at every meal. After Dad's finished, he stands and carves the ham.

"Help yourselves. There's plenty more in the kitchen," Mom says. "But leave some room for dessert. Anne made her cheese-cake-stuffed strawberries. They even look like little Santa hats. Wait until you see them." She grins and adds some ham to her plate.

Conversation flows easily, and I'm impressed with how much Hudson is sharing with my parents. He answers all my dad's pointed questions with ease. I can tell Dad approves, because he looks at me and nods. Too bad he's got the wrong idea.

The more I learn about Hudson, the more he's ticking off every box on my husband wish list. Strong, sensitive, funny, hardworking, intelligent.

Yep. I'm in trouble.

After dinner, I help Mom clear the table while Dad asks Hudson to come look at a door that doesn't want to close right.

"He's so wonderful, Anne," Mom says, drying the turkey plate I just washed. "I think you two are adorable together."

"Mom, stop." I roll my eyes. "We're literally just friends. Acquaintances, really."

She smiles. "Acquaintances don't sneak looks at each other throughout dinner, or lean on each other during church."

I blush. I'd somehow ended up leaning on Hudson's arm during the service. When I realized it, I moved to pull away, but he reached out and squeezed my hand. It felt nice, so I stayed.

"I think you're seeing things," I argue. "Hudson's not interested in settling down, Mom."

She grunts. "We'll see."

When the dishes are dry and put away, Mom and I join the guys in the living room. "My favorite part," Dad says, passing gifts to everyone, including two packages to Hudson.

"How does this work?" Hudson asks.

"We each take turns opening our gifts," I say. "Then we say something that we're thankful for this year."

He laughs. "I thought that was Thanksgiving?"

Mom nods. "We do it then, too. There's no bad time to be grateful."

Hudson tilts his head to the side as though he hadn't considered that before. "You're right. I like it."

One by one, we open gifts. Mom and Dad ooh and ahh over the basket of jams from Hudson. "Thank you."

"You're welcome," he says, blushing. "I hope you like them."

Dad pats his stomach. "Never met a jam I didn't like, son."

Hudson grins and nods. "Good to know, sir."

Next, they open their present from me. "Matching sweaters," Mom says, laughing. "This is perfect."

She holds hers up. It says "I'm Martha." I scoot over and pull Dad's from the box, holding it up so they can see. "I'm with Martha" is written across the back. "For when you go on your cruise to Alaska," I tell them.

Dad chuckles. "It's great. Thanks."

I stand and kiss each of them on the cheek. "Now, what are you grateful for this year?"

"I'm grateful for another year with my wonderful husband," Mom says, kissing Dad on the cheek.

"What about you, Dad?" I ask.

He doesn't respond right away, taking his time to really think it over. "I'm grateful for my health and my family."

"Your turn," I tell Hudson.

"Oh, I think I'd rather go last," he says. "If that's okay."

"Suit yourself," I say, grabbing the present from my parents first. I'm eager to know what Hudson got me, but as they say, curiosity killed the cat, so I save that one for last. I pull off the bright wrapping paper and slide my finger under the flap of the box. Popping the lid off, I grin when I see a brand new set of shears inside. "Thank you so much," I say, holding up the sleek black set. It's over the top, but it's so perfect.

"You're welcome," Dad says, smiling and squeezing Mom's knee.

Hudson clears his throat. "I wasn't sure what you might want, so I hope this is okay."

I carefully pull the tissue paper from the bag and open it. Inside is the cutest crocheted cat bum coaster set I've ever seen. Each one a unique pattern. I laugh and hold them up to show my parents.

"That's not all," Hudson says, pointing to the bag again.

I reach down inside and pull out a small box. I open it and gasp. Inside is a delicate chain with a rose-gold heart charm. "It's beautiful," I say, carefully removing it from the box. "Can you help me put it on?"

He rubs his hands on his slacks and moves behind me. "Sure."

Once it's clipped in place, Mom comes closer to look. "That's beautiful, Hudson. How'd you know she likes rose gold?"

He shrugs. "I noticed that's what she usually wears. I figured it was a safe bet."

Mom winks at me and mouths, "Told you so."

"So, what are you grateful for, Anne?" Dad asks.

I look around at the people in the room. "I think this year, I'm most grateful for friends and family."

"All right, Hudson. Your turn," Dad says.

He picks up the first box and unwraps the paper painfully slowly. "You can rip it, you know," I say, laughing.

He pins me with a serious look. "I don't like to rip it if I can help it. It's too pretty for that."

"Take your time," Mom says, breaking the tension in the air.

Hudson finally unwraps the box and opens it. "This is great!" He pulls out the long-sleeved shirt that says, "You've Got to be Kitten Me Right Meow," and laughs.

"I'm glad you like it," I say, smiling. It had been a toss-up between that shirt and a beanie that said, "Cattitude is everything."

"I love it." He folds the shirt back up and places it back in the box before moving to the next one.

Again, he unwraps it slower than a sloth trying to cross a road, and I'm wiggling impatiently.

He grins and holds up a handmade scarf in University of Arkansas colors. "This is awesome, thank you."

Mom leans into Dad and smiles. "You're welcome. I noticed your sweater the other day and figured you might like it."

He nods and wraps it around his neck. "I do, thank you. This has been the best Christmas Eve I've had in a long, long time, and that's what I'm grateful for."

I look around at the people in the room and smile. I couldn't agree more.

CHAPTER EIGHT

Hudson

LOOKING AROUND THE MASTERSES' house, it's clear that Dad and I could use a bit more spirit in our celebrations. There's always love, but other than the three-foot fake tree Dad's put up every year since I can remember, we don't use any decorations. Nothing that makes his house feel festive or . . . happy. Not like here, where everywhere I look, there's tinsel, or lights, or garland.

"I think I'm going to head home," Anne says, standing and brushing stray glitter from her dress. "Thank you, Daddy; Momma." She leans in and gives them each a kiss on the cheek.

"Don't forget your leftovers, dear," Martha says, cleaning up the last of the discarded wrapping paper.

"I'll walk out with you." I push to my feet to gather my things and say my goodbyes. "Thank you so much for inviting me, Mr. and Mrs. Masters." When Anne returns from the kitchen, two bags are dangling from her arm. "Looks like you'll be set for a while," I say, pointing at the bags.

Anne laughs and Martha shakes her head. "One of those is for you."

"Oh. Thank you." That warm, too big feeling is back in my chest. "You didn't have to do that."

Mr. Masters stands and holds out his hand. "It was a pleasure to meet you, Hudson. I hope to see you around here again."

"Thank you, sir. I appreciate that." I glance at Anne, and find myself hoping for more opportunities to spend time with her and her family.

"Call me Ronald or Ron." He grins. "Mr. Masters was my father." He chuckles at his own joke and settles back into his rocking chair. "Y'all be careful going home."

"Night, Daddy. Night, Mom. Thanks for everything." I take the bags, both of them, from Anne and follow her out the door.

"I think you made their night," Anne says when we step up to her car—a VW bug with eyelashes and little magnetic Christmas lights all along the side. It suits her perfectly.

"Oh, I think that had more to do with you. You're pretty amazing." I feel my face warm as the words slip out.

Anne's eyes fall to my chest before making their way back up to mine. "Thanks."

I'm not ready to end this night. The feeling is so unusual that it takes me a minute to recognize that's why my feet haven't moved. "Hey, are you busy in the morning?"

Anne's forehead creases as her eyebrows draw down. "No," she says finally.

"Want to help me decorate my dad's house? He has breakfast plans with his friend, who was recently widowed, and I think I'd like to surprise him with some Christmas cheer." It's not like Dad has always lacked Christmas spirit. Pictures from my early childhood years show him hanging lights, laughing by the tree with me in his lap, and a Santa hat perched atop his head.

"Oh, well . . ." She turns and places her bags in her back seat.

"Please," I ask. "I haven't really done much decorating before. I'll need some help." I grin and bring my hands together in front of me.

"Do you have decorations?" she asks, disbelief evident in her voice.

I nod. "I'm sure they're in the attic."

She thinks for a minute before she nods her head. "Okay, I'll help."

My heart leaps in my chest. "Thank you." I step back for her to get into her car. "I'll text you the address," I say before she closes the car door.

I stand in the driveway and watch her back out and pull away before letting free the smile I've been holding back. There's something about her that I can't put into words, but it draws me to her. I can't seem to erase her from my mind, and I'm not sure I want to.

I'm just bringing the last box down from the attic when I hear a car door shut out front. Hurrying to the living room, I set the box down and open the front door. "Thank you for coming," I say when Anne reaches the front steps. She's stunning. Her light brown hair is pulled up in a messy bun, a thick sweater with candy canes on it hangs down nearly to her knees, covering a pair of black leggings. "You look festive."

She smiles. "Thanks." She pulls the sweater away from her body and grins. "It's my Christmas sweater. The people at the nursing home love it." She steps inside and slips off her shoes, showing off a pair of candy cane-striped socks.

I pull up my pant leg, showing her my matching pair. "Seems we have something in common." She laughs, and the sound is like a gift to my heart. "You mentioned the nursing home ..."

"Oh, yeah. I go every year and visit with the residents. A lot of them don't get visitors this time of year, so I go and sit with them for a while. Sometimes we watch Christmas movies or play games." She smiles softly.

Why haven't I ever considered that? "That's really nice of you. Maybe I could go with you?"

She tilts her head, her eyebrows raised in surprise. "You'd want to go sit at a nursing home?"

"This might surprise you," I say in a half whisper, "but I do have a heart." I turn and step into the living room. "Here's all the boxes I found in the attic. I'm not sure what's in here, but there's bound to be some stuff we can use." When she doesn't answer, I turn and see she hasn't moved. "What's wrong?"

She shakes her head. "I'm sorry. I know you have a heart. It's just . . . no one's ever asked to go with me before." She walks into the living room, opens a box, and starts pulling things out.

"I'd like to go sometime, even if it's not today. I didn't think about people not getting visitors. That must be incredibly sad and lonely for them." I think of my dad. He's got his friends, but how lonely must he have been all these years?

I'm not so sure I want to be single for the rest of my life, anymore. I stop and watch Anne as she riffles through the box of miscellaneous decorations, a goofy grin on her face. Yeah. Staying single is less appealing these days.

"Oh my gosh," Anne says, giggling as she lifts something out of the box. "Is this you?" She turns the photo frame in my direction. A picture of toddler me sitting on my mom's lap, a giant stocking in front of us, faces me. "It is." I reach for the frame and study the photo. "I don't remember ever seeing this picture before."

She comes and stands beside me. "She's beautiful."

I swallow the lump in my throat. "She is." The same brown eyes I've been looking at in the mirror my whole life stare back at me from the most delicate face I've ever seen. I set the photo frame to the side to take home with me. "Did you find anything else?"

Anne nods and goes back to the box. "I found these," she says, holding up what appears to be several lengths of red and gold garland. "Have any tape to secure it?"

"If he does, it'll be in the junk drawer in the kitchen. I'll check." Dad's house is an older ranch style. Wide, arched doorways on either side of the sofa lead to the kitchen and dining room from the living room. Soft Christmas music starts in the living room, and I smile to myself. Leave it to Anne to think of playing carols while we decorate.

"Can I use the restroom?" Anne calls.

"Sure," I say, grabbing the tape from the junk drawer. "Down the hall—first door on the left."

The door to the bathroom clicks closed just as I enter the living room. A glance around the room leaves me stumped. Where are we going to use garland?

I'm pulling more things from the box when the front door swings open.

"What are you doing here so early?" Dad asks, stepping inside.

"I didn't expect you home so soon," I say, stepping in front of the open boxes. "I . . ."

Clearly, I'm not the wall I hoped I was because Dad crosses his arms over his chest and raises a brow—his signature look when he wants to know what I'm up to.

"Hi," Anne says, coming to stand beside me. "I'm Anne. Hudson's friend. We thought we'd surprise you with some Christmas joy this morning." She sticks out her hand. "You caught us." She giggles as Dad shakes her hand.

"Some Christmas joy, huh?" Dad asks, pulling his hand back and rubbing it along his jaw. "I didn't think you much liked Christmas, Hudson."

I shrug. "I don't think we ever gave it much thought." It's not like there was someone in our lives who loved to decorate. Dad's tastes were simple. Practical.

"It's nice to meet you, Anne. I'm Jake. Looks like you found the boxes. How can I help?" Dad steps around me and stops short. "Oh, I forgot about that," he says, picking up the frame.

"I can go put it in the truck," I say, reaching for it.

He shakes his head. "No, it's okay, son. It's a memory of a happier time."

Anne looks between the two of us and then claps her hands. "Well, let's get started, shall we? I have to leave in about an hour." She picks up a wreath she must have discovered while Dad and I were talking, and takes it and the door hanger to the front door.

"You're not going to stay for supper?" Dad asks. He takes three nutcrackers out of the box and places them on the coffee table.

"She goes to visit the nursing home residents in the afternoon," I answer. "It's her tradition."

Dad nods. "That's wonderful. We should go, too." Dad starts humming along with the music as though this whole interaction is normal for us.

"Sure," Anne says. "The more the merrier." She gives me a forced smile.

"We can go another time," I say, watching her face. "I hate to impose on another one of your traditions."

She frowns. "You're not imposing, but I'd hate for you two to change your plans. I thought you had your own traditions."

"We've been surviving," Dad fills in. "It's time to start living again. Don't you think, son?"

Who is this man, and what did he do with my father?

"Can I talk to you for a minute?" I ask, taking him by the arm and nearly dragging him into the kitchen. Once we are out of earshot, I cross my arms over my chest. "Okay, spill it. What aren't you telling me?"

Dad laughs. "What are you talking about? I'm not keeping anything from you."

I don't buy it. Not for a dollar, not for a quarter, not even for free. "Then where's all this coming from? I mean, I wanted to do something nice and surprise you, but I figured you'd be a bit upset. We haven't decorated for the holidays since Mom left."

He shakes his head. "That's not entirely true."

"Yes, it is," I counter.

He puts his hands on my shoulders. "No, it's not. The first few years after Mom left, I tried. My heart wasn't in it, but I tried. One year, you got upset and told me you hated Christmas and to stop trying to make it the same." He shrugs his shoulders and drops his head. "So, I didn't bring the decorations out again. I thought you'd ask for them back eventually, but you never did."

Memories of that Christmas come rushing back. I was a little kid. Mad because my mom wasn't here to bake cookies or take me to see Santa. "I remember that now. I'm sorry, Dad. The older I got, the more afraid I was to ask. I figured you were still hurting, and I didn't want to pour salt into your wounds."

Dad laughs at that. "Oh my. We aren't so good at communication, are we?" He pulls me in for a hug. "Son, your momma broke my heart, but hearts heal. I'm okay. I've been okay for a while now. In fact," he says, pausing and pulling away from me, "I've been seeing someone."

My jaw drops. I've entered another dimension. "You have?"

He nods. "I have. That's who I had breakfast with this morning." He blushes, and I can't help the laughter that bursts out of me.

"Why didn't you just tell me? I'm a grown man, Dad." I can't believe it. He's got a ... what? A girlfriend? That sounds too juvenile for an older man, but what else do you call it?

"I didn't know how you'd take it. I've been alone a long time, and I know you're anti relationships and marriage. Seemed like you might be upset, and after everything with your mom, and the few women I tried to date after ... I just wanted to be sure before I said anything."

My mouth goes dry. "Sure? As in ..."

He pulls out his phone and shows me a picture of a beautiful older woman. Laugh lines crinkle around her eyes as she looks at my dad with pure adoration. "I'm going to ask Lori to marry me."

My eyes snap to his. "What? When?"

"Soon," he blurts. "If that's okay. I want you to meet her first."

I nod. "If you love her, I'm sure I will, too."

He points to the living room. "So ... Anne?"

"I'm feeling that out," I say, hesitantly. "She makes me feel things. I want things with her that I never thought I wanted." I rub my hand over the ache in my chest. "I don't know what to do with that, or if she feels anything, but I think I'm ready to find out."

Dad grins and claps me on the back. "Then what are you doing in here talking to me? Get out there and show her you're worth taking a leap with."

He's right. What am I waiting for?

CHAPTER NINE

Anne

I'M HANGING BOWS ABOVE the doorway into the kitchen, when I catch the tail end of their conversation and nearly fall off the stool I found in the bathroom. Hudson has feelings for me?

He turns away from his father and spots me standing in the doorway. "Anne." My name is a whisper on his lips.

"I'm so sorry." I step down from the stool and back away. "I was just hanging decorations. I . . ." I have no idea what to say. I should have moved on to something else and come back to the bows later.

"It's okay," Hudson says, finally reaching me and taking my hands in his. "I know you weren't eavesdropping on purpose."

I shake my head. "I wasn't."

He tucks a stray hair behind my ear, his fingers lingering on the side of my face. "How much did you hear?"

A rush of warmth fills my cheeks. "The last part," I whisper, my eyes on his. Searching for the truth there. All this time, I'd thought he wasn't interested in me, so I'd pushed away the attraction I felt building.

His eyes are filled with hope, and maybe a bit of fear. He drops his hand to his side. "I guess the cat's out of the bag, then."

The sound of a door opening and closing reminds me we aren't alone. Unsure how to respond, I just stand there like I'm made of wax.

He chuckles nervously. "I like you, Anne. I've liked you since I met you months ago at Heath's birthday party. The more time I've spent with you, the more I like you. I can't stop thinking about you, and when I'm with you, I don't want it to end."

My eyes burn, and I'm afraid to blink, because I'm pretty sure I'll cry. "That's the sweetest thing I've ever heard," I say softly. "I like you, too. I always thought you weren't interested in me. You never asked me out, and Gabby said ..."

He nods. "I know. I didn't think I was meant to be in a relationship. Didn't think I wanted to let someone have that much hold over my heart, but with you ... It doesn't feel scary, or like I have a choice." He laughs. "So, what do you say? Can I take you out on a real date sometime?"

My heart warms. "I think I'd like that."

His smile lights up the room, and I'm giddy like a schoolgirl who got to put a checkmark on the "yes" box.

"Great. I'd love to take you out this weekend." He pulls out his phone and opens his calendar app. "Would Friday or Saturday be better?"

I laugh. *Is this real life?* "Um, Saturday. I'm off that day." Plus, I can get Gabby or Reese to come over and help me choose an outfit.

"Perfect." He slides the phone back into his pocket and picks up a Santa hat I'd set down on the coffee table. Putting it on his head, he says, "Ho, ho, ho. It's a Merry Christmas indeed."

The sound of someone clearing his throat makes us both turn, laughing, toward Jake, who's just come back into the room. "How about we leave this for later and go spread some Christmas cheer?"

He points to his clock. "I think it's about the time you wanted to head out?"

I look at my watch and grin. "Close enough. Come on, Santa. You can pass out the gifts."

Hudson's eyebrows draw together. "Gifts?"

I laugh. "Yeah, I get the residents a little something each year. The church chips in with donations."

He grins. "Next year, I'm donating, too."

My mind races ahead in time. Will this be something we do together next year as well? Do I want it to be?

It doesn't take but a second for me to realize that, yes, I want it to be *our* tradition.

After Hudson and Jake help me haul the bags of presents into the nursing home, we sign in with the front desk and head to the wing with patients who can't join us in the common room.

With each stop, Hudson cheerfully plays Santa, and his dad joins him. "These things are great," Hudson says, holding up a crocheted Christmas Gnome. "It's the perfect size for their bedside tables, or they can hold them in their hands."

I nod. "There's a women's group at church that works on them throughout the year. They also make baby hats and mittens for the hospital, and hats for cancer patients, too."

"Oh!" Hudson says. "I bet that's the one Heath's mom goes to. A support group or something?"

I nod. "I think so? I haven't been. While I may not have a creative streak, I do donate yarn a few times per year."

"I wonder if they have any groups for the men," Jake says. Hudson's mouth drops open. "You're going to let flies in, doing that."

I laugh. "I'm not sure, but I can ask my dad."

He nods and steps inside the next room.

After we've handed out a stuffed Christmas ornament to each resident, we move to the common room to join in the movie time. A Christmas Story is playing, and residents are relaxing all around the room. We take three empty chairs and settle in, laughing when one of the men relays a story of how he once got his tongue stuck to a light pole as well.

After the movie ends, we say our goodbyes and finish passing out the remaining gifts to the residents.

"This was amazing," Jake says when we step outside. "Thank you for letting us join you."

Hudson nods in agreement and interlaces his fingers with mine as he walks me to my car. "I'd like to come back and visit another time. I'm sure some of these residents would like more than just a Christmas visit."

"I'm glad you think so," I say, smiling. "I come one Saturday a month and give free haircuts. You're welcome to join me anytime."

"Please say you'll join us for dinner," Jake says, giving me a quick hug.

I glance at Hudson, who seems to be holding his breath in anticipation of my answer. "Okay," I say. "But you have to let me clean up after."

"No!" the men say in unison. "You're our guest," Hudson adds.

They don't look like they will budge on this point, so I decide to let it go. "Fine."

Their faces split into identical smiles. "Dinner should be ready at 6:30. You're welcome to come back over now, if you'd like."

After a minute, I shake my head. "No, thanks. I need to go home and check on Shelby. I'll be over around six, if that's okay?"

The men nod. "I can't wait," Hudson says, squeezing my fingers in his.

As I turn to slide into the driver's seat, I can't help but smile to myself. The warmth of Hudson's hand still lingers in mine, and for the first time in a long while, I feel a flutter of hope and excitement in my chest.

I glance back at Hudson, catching the soft look in his eyes. My heart skips a beat, and I realize that this might be the start of something I hadn't seen coming—something wonderful.

Shelby's lounging on the back of the sofa when I step into the apartment. I plop down on the couch and pull her onto my lap. "You'll never believe the day I've had," I say, stroking her soft fur.

My phone rings, and I snag it from my leggings pocket. Reese's name lights up the screen. "Merry Christmas," I say, answering.

"Merry Christmas. I was calling to see if you were certain you didn't want to join us for dinner. I hate the idea of you being alone on Christmas." Reese's concerned voice carries over the line and soothes a part of me that feels a bit wild at the moment.

"I'm sure," I say. "Besides, I won't be alone." The perma-smile I've been wearing since leaving the nursing home grows even bigger. "I'm having dinner with Hudson and his dad."

She gasps. "What? As friends or . . ."

I hesitate. "I think it's 'or.'"

"I thought he was a consummate bachelor?" she asks.

"Apparently not anymore." I explain what happened this morning, and she goes silent. "Reese?"

"Wow, that's a lot," she says. "How do you feel?"

"Like I'm in a dream," I answer. "I've liked him since I met him, but when nothing ever came of it, I let it go. Or tried to. The better I know him, the more good qualities I see in him." I take a deep breath and let it out slowly to calm my thoughts. "It's unexpected, but I think it's good."

"That's great! I'm thrilled for you," she says. "So, need help choosing an outfit for your date?"

After making plans for her to come over Saturday morning, we hang up. I sit on the couch for a while, listening to Shelby purr, her weight and warmth in my lap grounding me.

Things are changing, but maybe it's the type of change I've been wishing for.

I pull up to Jake's house a few minutes before six, nerves fluttering in my stomach. It's just dinner, I remind myself. With Hudson. And his dad. On Christmas.

No pressure.

I'm halfway up the walkway when the front door swings open, and Hudson steps out onto the porch. He's changed into a soft gray sweater that makes his shoulders look impossibly broad, and my heart does a little flip.

"Hey," he says, his signature goofy grin spreading across his face. "You came."

"I said I would."

"I know." He shoves his hands in his pockets, looking almost shy. "I'm just glad you did."

He holds the door open for me, and the smell of roasted turkey and something sweet—pie, maybe—wraps around me like a hug.

Jake's voice carries from the kitchen, warm and animated, followed by a woman's laughter.

Hudson's smile flickers. Just for a second, but I catch it.

"Dad's girlfriend is here," he says, his tone carefully neutral. "He wanted to invite her as well. Sorry I didn't tell you before."

"That's okay." I study his face, trying to read what's underneath the surface. "Is it okay with you?"

He hesitates, then nods. "Yeah. It's fine. She seems nice. I think she's good for him."

Before I can respond, Jake appears in the hallway, a dish towel slung over his shoulder. "Anne! Come in, come in." He ushers me toward the kitchen, where a woman with silver-streaked auburn hair is pulling a casserole dish from the oven.

"Anne, this is Lori," Jake says, and there's a softness in his voice I haven't heard before. "Lori, this is Hudson's Anne I've been telling you about."

Lori sets down the dish and wipes her hands on her apron before extending one to me. Her grip is warm and firm, her smile genuine. "It's so nice to finally meet you. Jake hasn't stopped talking about the wonderful young woman who brought Christmas to the nursing home today."

"It was a team effort," I say, glancing at Hudson. He's leaning against the doorframe, arms crossed, watching the exchange with an expression I can't quite decipher.

"Well, I think it's lovely," Lori says. "Jake mentioned you volunteer there regularly?"

I nod. "Once a month. Free haircuts for the residents."

"She's being modest," Hudson says, pushing off from the door-frame. "She's amazing with them."

The warmth in his voice makes my cheeks flush. "I just like helping people."

Lori's eyes dart between us, a knowing smile tugging at her lips. "I can see why Jake's so fond of you."

Dinner is delicious—turkey with all the fixings, green bean casserole, mashed potatoes covered in gravy, and rolls so fluffy they practically melt on my tongue. Lori, it turns out, is a retired schoolteacher who met Jake at a singles mixer two years ago.

The conversation flows easily enough—Jake asks about my family, Lori shares stories from her teaching days, and Hudson chimes in when prompted. But he's quieter than usual, and every now and then, I catch him staring out the window at nothing in particular.

After we've cleared the main course, Jake stands and stretches. "Lori and I will handle dessert. You two go relax for a few minutes."

"I can help—" I start, but Jake waves me off.

"Nonsense. You're our guest." He gives Hudson a pointed look. "Show her the back porch. The stars are beautiful tonight."

Hudson hesitates, then nods. "Yeah. Okay."

The back porch is small but charming. Two rocking chairs face a yard dotted with potted plants. The night air is crisp, carrying the faint scent of woodsmoke from a neighbor's chimney.

Hudson drops into one of the chairs and lets out a slow breath. I settle into the other one, tucking my legs beneath me.

For a moment, neither of us speaks. The silence isn't uncomfortable, but it's heavy with things unsaid.

"You okay?" I ask softly.

He doesn't answer right away. Just rocks the chair slowly, his eyes fixed on the lights twinkling in the trees.

"Yeah," he finally says. "I think so."

"You don't have to be, you know." I turn to face him. "It's okay if it's weird. Seeing your dad with someone else."

His jaw works, and I watch him wrestle with something internal. "It's not that I don't like her," he says slowly. "Lori's great. She makes him happy. Happier than I've seen him in years."

"But?"

He runs a hand through his hair. "But it's been just the two of us for so long. After Mom left . . ." He trails off, shaking his head. "I don't know. It's stupid."

"It's not stupid." I reach over and rest my hand on his arm. "Change is hard."

He looks down at my hand, then back up at me. "How do you do that?" he asks.

"Do what?"

"Make everything feel less complicated."

I laugh softly. "I don't think I do anything. I just listen."

"That's more than most people do." He turns his hand over and laces his fingers through mine. The warmth of his palm against mine sends a shiver up my spine that has nothing to do with the cold.

We sit like that for a while, rocking gently in the quiet, our breath making small clouds in the night air.

"She's good for him," Hudson says again, quieter this time. "And I want him to be happy. I just need to get used to it."

"You will." I squeeze his hand. "And for what it's worth, I think you're handling it really well."

He snorts. "I barely said two words the whole dinner."

"Well, we all know you're a regular chatterbox."

That earns me a real laugh, and the sound of it loosens the tightness in my chest.

The back door creaks open, and Jake pokes his head out. "I'm not interrupting am I? Pie's ready, if you two want to come back inside."

Hudson groans. "Dad."

"What?" Jake grins.

I duck my head to hide my smile as Hudson pulls me to my feet, his hand still wrapped around mine.

"Come on," he says, leading me back inside. "Before he embarrasses me any further."

But he's smiling when he says it, and I think—maybe—some of the weight has lifted from his shoulders.

CHAPTER TEN

Hudson

PURCASSO MEOWS LOUDLY AT my feet. "I see you," I say, filling his food dish. "You act like I never feed you." He winds himself between my legs as I bend down and place his dinner on the floor. "Be good," I say, patting his head.

My stomach is a ball of knots. I take a deep breath and grab my wallet and keys. I've been on dates before, but I've never been this nervous. Locking the door behind me, I make my way to the truck. Joy, the owner of Blooming Joy flower shop, helped me pick out a bouquet of mixed flowers. I didn't want to give her roses on our first date—too cliche.

The drive to her apartment feels agonizingly long, even though it's only twenty minutes. What if she changed her mind? It's happened before. When women realized I meant it when I said I wasn't looking to settle down, they usually canceled on me.

For the first time, I find myself hoping this date leads to more. And not just more dates, either. With Anne, I could picture the whole shebang—marriage, cute little kids with my sense of humor and her good looks. I want it all.

I've heard people say "when you know, you know," but I always thought it was a way to justify how fast they moved. Now I see what they mean.

I pull into a parking space, put the truck in park, grab the flowers, and hop out. I take the steps two at a time and knock on the door.

The door swings open, and I'm speechless. Anne is radiant in a red sweater and dark blue jeans. Her hair is done in some complicated twist, and her lips are a shimmery red to match her top. I wonder what it would feel like to press my lips to hers.

"Hello," she says, shifting her weight from side to side. "Are those for me?"

I blink my eyes hard. "Yes, sorry." She steps to the side, and I hand her the bouquet as I enter her space for the first time. "You look beautiful."

She blushes. "Thanks. I'll just put these in some water," she says, lifting the bouquet up between us.

While she runs the faucet and fills a vase, I look around. Her style is eclectic, but cozy. Colorful throw pillows line the back of the couch where a chunky cat is fast asleep. The window is adorned with sparkle lights, and a small Christmas tree is placed on a table in the corner.

"I'm ready when you are," she says, capturing my attention.

"Lead the way," I say, following her out the front door. I hold her hand as we walk down the stairs and make sure to open the car door for her. Dad would be proud. He sat me down after Anne left on Christmas Day and gave me some tips. Apparently, he's learned a lot over the years. Both what not to do, and a few things that make a woman feel special, too.

Once we're both in the truck and headed to Surfside, I feel something inside me settle. "So, what kind of music do you like?"

She smiles. "Nearly anything, but my favorite is pop music. It's fun to dance to."

I envision her dancing around her apartment and grin. "Pop it is."

We sing along to the songs on the radio, and I sneak peeks at her when I think she's not looking, but she keeps catching me.

When we get to the restaurant, I'm pleasantly surprised by the atmosphere. I messaged Bradley yesterday and asked him where I should take her. This is one of his and Aurora's favorites, so I decided to give it a shot.

"This is gorgeous," Anne says, looking around the dining room. "How'd you get a reservation so fast?"

I shrug. "I got lucky, I think."

We both take our time looking at the menu and decide on the special when the waiter offers it.

"So," Anne says, folding her hands in her lap. "What are your hobbies?"

"I enjoy reading, and hiking. Anything outdoors really. What about you?" I take a drink of my water and grab a slice of bread from the basket.

"I like to volunteer at the nursing home, as you know already. I also like to read, but I don't like non-fiction books. Other than that, it's mostly work that takes up my time." She reaches over and takes a slice of bread for herself, buttering it before taking a bite and placing it on her plate.

"I prefer urban fantasy or science fiction, myself."

She lights up at that. "I love sci-fi, too," she says, then starts listing her current favorite books and asks if I've read them.

The waiter drops off our food, and we continue to share about ourselves as we eat.

"Did you always know you'd be in Piney Brook?" Anne asks.

I shrug. "Yeah. I never really thought about moving somewhere else." I don't tell her that I couldn't leave my dad alone. Not after Mom left him. He'd been so broken. "What about you?"

She pauses, and finishes her bite before shaking her head. "In beauty school, I had dreams of moving to the big city—celebrity clients, a penthouse in the city. I did an internship in New York, and I felt like a ghost. No one new my name, or asked how I was. I felt like a fraud, and I missed my friends and my parents."

"That must have been hard," I say, reaching out to touch her hand.

"When my aunt said she wanted to retire and offered the business to me, it felt like the right thing to do. I was relieved to come back home, honestly."

After that, the conversation flows freely, without any awkward silences, and when the waiter asks if we'd like dessert, and Anne declines, I find myself disappointed that the night's coming to a close.

"Thank you for dinner," she says when we're back in the car on the way home. "It was delicious. I've never been to Surfside before. It's a bit out of the way, and pricey for just me."

I smile and reach for her hand. "I'm glad you enjoyed it." The feel of her fingers between mine is so right it makes me want to never let go.

Too soon, we're back at her apartment, and I'm walking her to the door. "I had a great time tonight," I say while she unlocks her door.

"I did, too." The overhead light is just bright enough for me to catch the blush that stains her cheeks.

"Bradley and Aurora are having a New Year's Eve get-together. Would you like to go—as my girlfriend?" My heart stops, and blood pulses in my ears while I wait for her to answer.

She nods, and my heart takes flight and leaves my body. "I'd love to."

This is usually the part of the date where I kiss the lady on the cheek and send her inside, but I don't want to let her go. "Can I kiss you?"

She hesitates, and I worry I've pushed her too fast, so I stammer out, "It's okay. Another ..." I can't finish my sentence because the sweetest lips I've ever had the pleasure of tasting are pressed against mine.

A soft hum registers in the back of my mind, and I realize it's me making that noise. She pulls away, a dreamy look on her face that I'm sure is mirrored on mine. "Goodnight, Hudson."

"Goodnight," I say, my voice huskier than normal.

I watch her walk inside and shut the door, taking my heart with her.

New Year's Eve seems too far away. I sit in my truck for a long moment thinking about how much things have changed. For years, I convinced myself I wasn't the type to settle down. I viewed family as a responsibility I didn't want to carry. I never allowed myself to feel this much, too afraid of getting hurt. But watching the light flick on in Anne's apartment, and her shadow pass by the front window, makes those old fears disappear.

The conversation with my dad at Christmas comes rushing back. He was able to heal, move on ... love again. If he can let go of the hurt, and grasp at a chance for happiness, then so can I.

When you know you know. I hated that expression for so long. Now, I completely understand it. I pull out of the parking lot and head back home, a smile on my lips and a sense of rightness in my chest. Anne isn't girlfriend material. She's the whole shebang—the marriage, the kids, and the home I never thought I'd have. Most people would think I was insane for meeting with her dad and asking his permission to marry his daughter before I even took her on our first official date, but this ... us ... it's right, and I think I've known it since I met her at Heath's birthday party.

New Year's Eve can't come fast enough, because every second I'm away from her feels like a second of my life wasted.

Monday after work, I head to Bradley's to help him get ready for the New Year's Eve party tomorrow night. We're putting up tents in the backyard and setting up the tables and chairs. Thankfully, the snow's melted, and the forecast doesn't call for anymore of the fluffy white stuff. Otherwise he'd have a bunch of people squeezed into his little duplex apartment.

"So, how was your date?" Bradley asks, as we get the last pop-up tent in place.

"It was amazing." I grin. "Best date I've ever been on."

He laughs. "Your face right now ... But seriously, that's great. I'm happy for you."

"Hey, can I ask you a question?" I've asked my dad, but a second opinion never hurts.

"Shoot." Bradley drags a table under the tent and starts opening the legs.

"How soon is too soon to pop the question?"

Bradley jumps and drops the table on his foot. Jumping around in a circle, he lets out a string of colorful language.

"Are you okay?" I manage to ask between fits of laughter.

He shakes his head. "You made me break my foot." He gingerly steps on it and winces.

"Is it really broken?" I ask, my laughter dying off.

"No, but warn someone, would you?" He shakes his head and grabs the table, flipping it upright and setting it in place. "To answer your question, I think it depends on the couple. Some people are ready right away, others need more time to fall in love and feel right about it."

I slide another table over and set it up while I think that over. "So, now's too soon, then?"

He laughs. "You've been on one date. Are you sure you're ready to take such a big step?"

When he notices I'm not laughing along, he stops and looks at me. "She's it for me." I don't know how I know, I just do. "

"Is she ready for you to ask her?"

That's a good question, and one I don't have the answer to. "I'm not sure."

He nods. "Take your time. When it feels right, you'll know."

An hour later, we've finished setting everything up, and Aurora's decorated the inside. "It's going to be so much fun," she says, kissing Bradley on the cheek when he grumbles about the glitter that's fallen off the decorations and onto the floor. "I'll help you clean up the mess."

He pulls her close for a kiss and smiles. "You're right."

That.

Right there.

I want that. With Anne. Forever.

And as far as I'm concerned. Forever can't come soon enough.

Chapter Eleven

Anne

THE BELL ABOVE THE salon door jingles, and I don't even have to look up to know it's him. Hudson walks in, balancing two cups from the Coffee Loft and a brown paper bag that smells a lot like burgers and french fries.

"I come bearing gifts of food," Hudson says, placing the haul on the counter.

"Is that from Beats and Eats?" I ask, nodding toward the bag as I finish up Mrs. Lopez's trim.

"You know it," Hudson says. "I got you a cheeseburger. Hope that's okay." He gives me that lopsided grin that makes my heart melt. "I'm just going to wash up while you finish up," he says, walking to the small restroom at the back of the salon.

"That young man is a keeper," Mrs. Lopez says, as she inspects her hair. "No dry today, dear."

"Are you sure?" I ask. "It's no problem."

She raises an eyebrow and points a perfectly manicured finger at me. "You have lunch with a handsome gentleman caller. Don't make him wait."

"Even I won't argue with that," I say. I ring her up and watch as she leaves the store, waving at someone across the street.

"I thought she'd never leave," Hudson says, pulling me in for a quick hug.

I laugh. "She had an appointment, and you're early."

He shrugs. "I couldn't wait." If his words didn't completely flip my heart upside down, the slight blush staining his cheeks does.

"Let's eat," I say, my voice a little breathless. Since our date, it seems neither one of us can stay away from the other for very long.

My journal sits open in front of me. This year's resolutions staring me in the face.

Spend more time with friends. Check.

Practice gratitude each day. Check

Drink more water. Well . . . I tried.

Volunteer more. Check

Find someone worth loving.

Do I check that one off? It seems way too early to be in love. Doesn't it?

I think back over the last few months. Meeting Hudson at Heath's birthday party. Spending time with him when Heath and Gabby invited us both over. Seeing him at Christmastime with my parents and his dad. Laughing with him while he showered the nursing home residents with kindness and cheer.

Our first date was magical. Like we were connected in a way that is unexplainable. When we kissed, I felt weightless, like the cares of the world floated away and were replaced with warmth and security. Like being wrapped in a warm blanket on a cold day.

Since our dinner at Surfside, Hudson has been a constant in my life. Showing up at my work with a coffee from the Coffee Loft. Bringing me lunch from Beats and Eats. It's sweet, and a whirlwind, but I don't want things to slow down. Things are moving at warped speed, and it should scare me, but it doesn't.

Too soon or not, I think I'm in love with Hudson Parks.

My hands shake so badly with the realization that I drop my pen.

I'm in love with Hudson.

My thoughts skip ahead to our date tonight. Our first official outing as a couple. I can't let him know that I've fallen for him. It would freak him out.

Until recently, he was adamant he was never getting married.

Maybe he still feels that way . . .

No, that doesn't make sense. He wouldn't pursue me if that were true. Right? He knows I want to settle down, have kids and a house. He agreed with me when I mentioned it at Surfside.

I take a deep breath. I'm getting worked up and putting the cart before the horse, as they say. One step at a time.

I pick up my pen and draw a check mark next to the last item.

Find someone to love. Check.

Now to write my new resolutions. Drink more water, of course. Find a new hobby. Spend more time outdoors. I pause when the last one comes to mind. Should I write it, or not?

I sit back in the chair and think. It's not like I haven't completed my resolutions before. Worst case scenario, it doesn't happen, right? But what if it does?

I nod to myself, steeling my resolve to boldly state what I want.

See where this goes with Hudson.

Immediately, I'm dreaming of us getting married and start a family—the white dress, my father walking me down the aisle. My chest feels bubbly. Like a pop can that's been shaken up. I could see it. Walking down the aisle to Hudson's big grin. Making a home together with kids running around the front yard. I feel like a middle schooler writing my crushes last name as my own.

Sighing, I close my journal, and stand. My stomach grumbles, and I realize I've missed lunch. Too busy daydreaming of things that might not even happen. I pad to the kitchen and make myself a tuna sandwich, putting a spoonful of tuna on a plate for Shelby. I add some baby carrots, and a handful of raspberries to my plate, my mom's voice ringing in my ears. *You need to have complete meals to stay healthy, Anne.* She never was a fan of my grazing habits.

After I scarf down my sandwich, I make my way to the bedroom to get ready for our date. I only have a few hours to decide on what to wear to what I hope will be my last first date.

The house is full of chatter and laughter when we step inside. Hudson guides me to the living room where Bradley, his boss, and his girlfriend Aurora are standing talking to an older couple I don't recognize.

"Hey," he says, getting their attention. "I'd like you to officially meet Anne, my girlfriend."

Aurora pulls me in for a hug. "It's about time this one decided to settle down."

He laughs. "Hey, now. You've only known me for a few months."

She nods. "And you've needed a woman in your life for at least that long," she says before breaking out into laughter.

"I'd like you to meet the owner of Lost Creek Construction, and this knucklehead's boss," Bradley says, motioning to the older gentleman. "Allen and Brenda Miller."

After chatting for a few minutes, we make our way outside where more people are sitting around tables and mingling. Tall heaters are strategically positioned in the yard, emitting enough heat to create a cozy outdoor atmosphere. Plates of appetizers are arranged on buffet tables, with stacks of small paper plates at either end.

"Let's get some food," Hudson says, passing me a paper plate and a napkin.

We stack our plates with finger foods and find two seats open at the back table. I sit down, and Hudson sits next to me. "Thanks for coming tonight," he says, leaning close to me so I can hear him over the chatter. The feel of his breath on my neck makes me shiver. "Are you cold?"

"No," I say, taking a bite of a mini taco.

Heath and Gabby join us first, and more people follow them until our table is full and bustling with conversation. After several rounds of UNO, and some more food, I cover my mouth and yawn.

"Are you tired?" Hudson asks, laying his hand on mine. "I can take you home if you're ready."

I shake my head. "I'm good. I'm a little sleepy, but I want to stay and watch the ball drop. It's already 11:30, another thirty minutes won't be too much."

He leans over and kisses my cheek. "If you're sure."

"I am," I say. Realizing we've drawn an audience, I turn my attention back to the table.

"So, you two serious, or what?" Heath asks, popping a mini quiche into his mouth.

"Heath!" Gabby squeaks.

"What? I'm just curious what his intentions are." He pins Hudson with a stare. "Anne is a good friend, and we both know she's the kind of woman you marry."

I stand. "Thank you, Heath, but I can take care of myself." My cheeks heat, though from embarrassment or anger, I can't be sure.

"It's okay," Hudson says, taking my hand in his and tugging me back down into my seat. "I can answer him."

My head whips toward him so fast, I'm certain I just gave myself whiplash. "You really don't have to," I say, pleading with my eyes for him to let this dream carry on a bit longer before he calls it off. I'm enjoying being in love.

"I know, but I want to." He turns toward Heath. Squeezing my hand once and relaxing. "I plan to marry her."

"What?!" Gabby and I both shriek at the same time.

Heath is grinning like a goon, and Hudson holds up his hand. "I love her. I can't explain it, and I don't want to. She's it for me. I think I've known it since the first time we talked at Heath's birthday party. When she's ready, I plan to put a ring on her finger and give her my last name. If she wants it, that is," he says, looking at me. "Whenever you're ready."

My mouth hangs open, and I can't find the strength to close it.

"I guess I should have told you first, huh?" he says, gently closing my mouth and placing a soft kiss on my cheek. "Sorry about that. I'm still new to all this."

"You love me?" I ask, my voice sounding distant to my own ears.

He smiles softly, his eyes twinkling. "I do."

"You want to marry me?"

He nods and takes both of my hands in his. "More than anything."

I swallow hard. "You'll have to ask my dad," I say, my mind reeling and reaching for anything to make time slow down for a second so I can bask in this feeling.

"I already did when we met for lunch last week," Hudson says. He leans over and kisses me on the forehead. "He said yes, by the way."

I'm stunned. This man, this beautiful, smart, funny man loves me.

"Okay," I say, finally.

He kisses my lips softly. "When you're ready. I'm not rushing you."

I nod and lick my lips. "I'm ready," I whisper.

Now it's his turn to be stunned silent, apparently. "Seriously?" he asks.

"Seriously. I love you, too, Hudson."

The whoop he lets out draws the attention from everyone outside. "You just made my New Year's wish come true!"

Laughing, I lean in and give him a kiss. "You are my wish come true."

"It's nearly midnight," Bradley calls. "Everyone inside for the ball drop."

We make our way inside, and Hudson wraps his arm around me.

"Ten. Nine. Eight . . ." Everyone is chanting. Hudson removes his arm, and I keep counting with everyone else. "Seven. Six. Five. Four . . ." At one, I turn to kiss Hudson, only to find he's down on one knee with a ring box open, and the most beautiful cushion-cut rose-gold ring nestled inside.

"Will you marry me?" he asks over the noise in the room.

I can't seem to find my voice, so I nod my head yes. He slips the ring on my finger and stands up. He places a soft kiss on my lips, and cheers go up from those around us who have caught on to what just happened.

"I need to hear it," he whispers against my lips. "Please?"

"Yes," I shout, making everyone laugh.

He grins and kisses me like it's the only thing he's ever wanted to do. Tender and sweet, his lips brush across mine and I shiver. He holds me closer, and it's like the whole room melts away, leaving just the two of us and our love.

Chapter Twelve

Hudson

Anne's apartment smells like vanilla and cinnamon when I walk through the door. She's got candles burning on the coffee table and something in the oven that's making my stomach growl.

"Smells amazing in here," I say, dropping my keys on the counter and crossing to where she's curled up on the couch with Shelby in her lap. I lean down and kiss her, then scratch behind Shelby's ears. "What's the occasion?"

"No occasion." She smiles up at me. "Just felt like baking. There's a lasagna in the oven and brownies cooling on the counter."

"You're going to spoil me."

"That's the plan."

I settle onto the couch beside her, and she shifts so her legs are draped across my lap. Shelby gives me a look of mild annoyance before relocating to the armchair across the room.

"So," Anne says, a teasing glint in her eye. "I was thinking we should probably talk about the wedding."

My stomach does a little flip. We've been engaged for two months now, and every time the wedding comes up, I feel a mix of excitement and low-grade panic. Not because I don't want to marry her—I've never wanted anything more—but because weddings big. Full of expectations I'm not sure I know how to meet.

"Okay," I say, trying to sound casual. "What are you thinking?"

She tucks a strand of hair behind her ear, and I can tell she's been rehearsing this. "Well, I know some people dream about big weddings with hundreds of guests and ice sculptures and five-tier cakes ..."

I cringe. "Please tell me you don't want an ice sculpture."

She laughs. "No ice sculptures. That's my point." She shifts to face me more fully, her green eyes soft and earnest. "I don't need any of that, Hudson. I just need you."

Something loosens in my chest. "Yeah?"

"Yeah." She reaches out and takes my hand, threading her fingers through mine. "What would you think about something small? Really small. Like, courthouse small."

I blink. "Courthouse?"

"Just us, our parents, and our best friends. Gabby as my maid of honor. Heath as your best man." She squeezes my hand. "Simple. Intimate. No fuss."

For a moment, I don't know what to say. Part of me feels a rush of relief so strong it nearly knocks the wind out of me. No crowd of people staring at me. No pressure. Just Anne and the people we love most.

But another part of me hesitates.

"Are you sure?" I ask. "I mean, this is your wedding. Don't most women want the big dress and the fancy venue and all the things?"

"The what?" She raises an eyebrow. "The stress? The year of planning? The passive-aggressive opinions from relatives I haven't seen since I was twelve?"

"When you put it that way."

"Hudson." She scoots closer, her hand coming up to rest on my cheek. "I've thought about this. A lot. And what I want is to marry you. I don't need to throw a party or try to impress the town. I just want to be your wife."

My throat tightens. "You're sure you won't regret it? Not having the big day?"

"I'm sure." Her thumb traces along my jaw. "Besides, the big day is whatever day I get to marry you. The rest is just details."

I turn my head and press a kiss to her palm. "I don't deserve you."

"Probably not," she says, grinning. "But you're stuck with me now."

I pull her onto my lap, and she laughs as Shelby meows in protest from across the room. "A courthouse wedding," I say, testing the words. "I have to admit, it sounds pretty perfect."

"Right? We can do it next month if we want. No waiting a year and a half for a venue."

"Next month?" My eyebrows shoot up. "That soon?"

She shrugs, but I can see the hopeful glimmer in her eyes. "Why wait? Unless you want more time."

"No." The word comes out faster than I intended. "No, I don't want more time. I've wasted enough time already."

Her smile could light up the whole apartment. "So, next month?"

"Next month," I agree. "But I'm still getting you flowers. And a cake. And whatever else you want."

"Brownies count as cake, right?"

"Anne."

"Fine, fine. We'll get a real cake." She taps her chin thoughtfully. "Something small, though. Maybe just a two-tier."

"What flavor?"

"Chocolate. Obviously."

"Obviously," I echo, grinning. "What about the dress? Please tell me you're still doing the dress."

She tilts her head. "Would it disappoint you if I didn't?"

"A little," I admit. "I've been picturing you walking toward me in white longer than I'd like to admit."

Her cheeks flush pink. "Since when?"

I think back to that night at McFadden's. The way she looked at me in the parking lot. The way I almost kissed her and didn't. All the months after, pretending I wasn't falling for her when I absolutely was.

"Since the beginning," I say quietly. "I just didn't let myself think about it."

She leans in and kisses me softly. "Then I'll wear a dress. A simple one. Something I can actually move in."

"You could wear a potato sack and you'd still be the most beautiful woman I've ever seen."

"Flattery will get you everywhere, Mr. Parks."

"That's the plan, future Mrs. Parks."

She grins and settles against my chest, her head tucked under my chin. We sit like that for a while, the apartment quiet except for the soft hum of the oven timer counting down.

"We should tell our parents," Anne says after a moment. "Before we make any final plans."

A knot forms in my stomach. Not because I'm worried about their reactions—I'm pretty sure they'll be thrilled—but because telling them makes it real. Official. Like we're actually doing this.

Which we are. And I want to. More than anything.

"What if we invited them all over?" I suggest. "Tell everyone at once. Rip off the Band-Aid."

Anne lifts her head, a slow smile spreading across her face. "I love that idea. This weekend?"

"This weekend."

Saturday afternoon, Anne's apartment is buzzing with activity. She's spent the morning cleaning and prepping snacks—a cheese board, those little spinach puff things she knows my dad loves, and a fresh batch of her famous brownies. I've been relegated to "stay out of the way" duty, which mostly involves sitting on the couch with Shelby and trying not to steal food.

"Stop picking at the cheese," Anne calls from the kitchen without even looking.

"I wasn't."

"You were. I heard you."

I pop one more cube of cheddar into my mouth before responding. "You're scary, you know that?"

"And don't you forget it."

The doorbell rings at exactly two o'clock. Anne's parents are first.

"Sweetheart!" Martha pulls Anne into a hug while Ron shakes my hand firmly.

"Good to see you, son," he says, and the casual way he calls me "son" still catches me off guard. In the best way.

"You too, sir."

"Ron," he corrects, like he always does. "Or Dad. We're going to be family. No need for formalities."

Before I can respond, another knock sounds at the door. I open it to find Dad and Lori on the doorstep, Lori holding a pie dish covered in foil.

"We brought pecan pie," she announces, pressing a kiss to my cheek as she sweeps past me. "I know it's your favorite."

Dad claps me on the shoulder and grins. "You look nervous. Why do you look nervous? She already said yes."

"Thanks for the support, Dad."

He laughs and follows Lori inside.

For the next twenty minutes, the apartment is filled with overlapping conversations and laughter. Martha and Lori hit it off immediately, bonding over their shared love of gardening and their mutual exasperation with "the men in their lives." Ron and Dad discover they both served in the military—different branches, different decades, but enough common ground to keep them talking.

Anne catches my eye from across the room and raises an eyebrow. *Ready?*

I nod.

She clears her throat. "So, we actually invited you all here for a reason."

The room goes quiet. Four pairs of eyes turn toward us expectantly.

"We've been talking about the wedding," Anne continues, reaching for my hand. "And we've made some decisions."

"Oh, here we go," Martha says, clutching Ron's arm. "I knew it. You're eloping, aren't you? Running off to Vegas without us?"

"Mom, no." Anne laughs. "Well, not exactly."

I squeeze her hand and jump in. "We want to keep things small. Really small. A courthouse ceremony with just the four of you, plus Gabby and Heath."

Silence.

I watch their faces, trying to read their reactions. Martha's eyes are wide. Ron looks thoughtful. Dad's expression is un-readable, and Lori has her hand pressed to her chest.

"That's . . ." Martha starts, then stops. Her eyes are glistening. "That's perfect."

"Really?" Anne sounds surprised. "You're not disappointed? I know you always talked about walking me down the aisle in a church."

"Sweetheart." Martha crosses the room and takes Anne's face in her hands. "I don't care if you get married in a church or a courthouse or the middle of a cornfield. I just want you to be happy." She glances at me. "And I can see that you are."

Ron nods in agreement. "What matters is the marriage, not the wedding. You two know what you want, and that's all that counts."

I feel a lump forming in my throat and turn to Dad. He's been quiet, watching the exchange with a soft expression I don't see often.

"Dad? What do you think?"

He stands and walks over to us, his eyes moving between me and Anne. For a long moment, he doesn't say anything. Then he pulls me into a hug.

"I think," he says gruffly, "that you're making the right choice. Both of you." He pulls back and looks at Anne. "Welcome to the family. Officially."

Anne's eyes are shining. "Thank you, Jake."

Lori joins us, wrapping an arm around Dad's waist. "We're so happy for you both. And honestly? A small ceremony sounds lovely. More intimate. More *you*."

"That's what we thought," Anne says, leaning into me.

"So when's the big day?" Ron asks, rubbing his hands together. "Do we have a date?"

Anne and I exchange a look.

"Next month," I say. "If that works for everyone."

Martha gasps. "Next month? That's so soon!"

"We don't want to wait," Anne says simply. "We know what we want."

Another beat of silence. Then Martha breaks into a grin.

"Well then. We'd better get planning." She turns to Lori. "We'll need to coordinate outfits. Nothing too matchy-matchy, but complementary, don't you think?"

And just like that, the two moms are off, huddled together and chattering about colors and flowers and whether the courthouse has good natural lighting. Ron and Dad drift toward the cheese board, debating the merits of different meat and cheese pairings.

Anne tugs me toward the kitchen, away from the happy chaos.

"That went well," she whispers.

"Better than well." I wrap my arms around her waist. "They're happy for us."

"Of course they are." She rises on her tiptoes and kisses me softly. "We're pretty great together."

"The greatest."

She rolls her eyes but she's smiling. "Don't let it go to your head."

From the living room, I hear Dad laugh at something Ron said, followed by Lori's delighted squeal over some wedding detail. Our families, blending together like they've known each other for years instead of months.

This is what I almost walked away from. What I almost convinced myself I didn't deserve.

"Hey." Anne's voice pulls me back. "Where'd you go?"

I shake my head. "Nowhere. Just thinking about how lucky I am."

She studies my face for a moment, then smiles a soft, knowing smile that makes me feel like she can see straight through me.

"We're both lucky," she says.

And for the first time in my life, I actually believe it.

"What do you think Heath will say when you ask him to be your best man?" she asks.

I snort. "He'll probably say 'I told you so.' Repeatedly. For the rest of our lives."

"He did call it early."

"Don't remind me." I think about all the times Heath nudged me toward Anne. All the knowing looks and not-so-subtle comments. The man's going to be insufferable at the wedding. "He's going to cry, you know. During the ceremony."

"Heath? No way."

"Oh, absolutely. He's a secret softie. Gabby's turned him into a puddle."

Anne laughs. "Well, Gabby's definitely going to cry. She teared up just looking at my ring."

"We're going to be surrounded by weeping people."

"As long as it's happy weeping," she says. "That's the best kind."

I press a kiss to the top of her head. "If you say so."

The oven timer beeps, and Anne reluctantly untangles herself from my arms. "Dinner's ready. You hungry?"

"Starving."

She heads to the kitchen, and I watch her go, still marveling at the fact that this is my life now. That this woman—this kind, funny, beautiful woman—wants to marry me.

A year ago, I would've run from this. Would've convinced myself I didn't deserve it, didn't want it, couldn't handle it.

Now I can't imagine wanting anything else.

"Hey," I call after her. "What about a honeymoon? Any thoughts?"

She peeks around the corner, oven mitts on her hands. "Somewhere warm. With a beach. And no cell service."

"No cell service?"

"I want you all to myself for at least a week, Hudson Parks. No distractions."

I grin. "I think that can be arranged."

Courthouse wedding. Next month. Anne in a white dress, walking toward me.

I can picture it so clearly it makes my chest ache.

And for the first time since my mom left, the future doesn't feel like something to fear. It feels like something to run toward.

Epilogue

HUDSON

NOTHING COULD'VE PREPARED ME for this moment.

I'm standing in a small room at the Piney Brook courthouse, tugging at my tie for the hundredth time, when Heath claps a hand on my shoulder.

"You're going to strangle yourself if you keep doing that."

"It's too tight."

"It's the same tie you wore to my engagement party." He raises an eyebrow. "It fit fine then."

"Well, it doesn't fit now."

Heath laughs and bats my hands away, adjusting the knot with practiced ease. "There. Perfect." He steps back and looks me over. "You clean up nice, Parks."

"Thanks." I take a breath and try to calm the herd of wild horses stampeding through my chest. "Is she here yet?"

"Gabby just texted. They're pulling into the parking lot." Heath grins. "Last chance to run."

"Not a chance."

And I mean it. Every word.

Six months ago, I would have laughed if someone told me I'd be standing here, minutes away from getting married. I'd spent most of my adult life avoiding commitment, vulnerability, the risk of loving someone enough to let them hurt me.

Then Anne walked into my life and rewrote every rule I'd ever made for myself.

Dad appears in the doorway, Lori beside him. His eyes are suspiciously bright. "They're ready for you, son."

I nod and follow him out into the hallway. The courthouse isn't fancy—just a simple room with wooden benches and tall windows that let in the late afternoon light. But Anne wanted simple. She wanted *us*. And that's exactly what this is.

I take my place at the front of the room, Heath standing beside me. On the other side of the aisle, Gabby is already in position, a small bouquet of wildflowers in her hands. She catches my eye and winks.

Our parents fill the front row—Dad and Lori on one side, Anne's mom and a space for her dad on the other. Martha is already dabbing at her eyes with a tissue.

This is it. This is my family. Not just the one I was born into, but the one I'm choosing.

The door at the back of the room opens, and everything else falls away.

Anne steps through, and I forget how to breathe.

She's wearing a simple white dress—no train, or veil, just soft fabric that flows to her knees and catches the light when she moves. Her hair is down, loose waves cascading over her shoulders. She's holding a small bouquet of peonies, and she's smiling.

At me. She's smiling at *me*.

My vision blurs, and I blink hard. I am not going to cry. I am *not* going to—

A tear slips down my cheek.

Okay. I'm crying. Heath is never going to let me live this down.

But I don't care. Because Anne is walking toward me, her eyes locked on mine, and she's the most beautiful thing I've ever seen.

Ron walks her down the aisle, her arm looped through his. When they reach me, he stops and looks me dead in the eye.

"Take care of her," he says, his voice low and steady.

"With everything I have," I promise.

He nods, satisfied, and places Anne's hand in mine. Her fingers are trembling slightly, and I realize she's nervous too. Somehow, that makes me feel better.

"Hi," she whispers.

"Hi." I squeeze her hand. "You look incredible."

"You're crying."

"I'm not crying. It's allergies."

She laughs softly, and the sound settles something in my chest. This is right. This is exactly where I'm supposed to be.

The officiant begins the ceremony, but I barely hear the words. I'm too focused on Anne. Her thumb traces soothing circles on my palm, as she looks at me like I'm the only person in the room.

When it's time for the vows, I take a shaky breath.

"Anne." My voice comes out rougher than I intended. "I spent a long time believing I wasn't meant for this." I swallow hard. "And then I met you. And you didn't just change my mind—you changed my whole life."

Her eyes are glistening now, and I push on.

"You're the kindest person I know. The most patient. The most forgiving." I shake my head slowly. "I don't know what I did to deserve you, but I promise to spend every day trying to be worthy of you. I promise to be there for the good days and the hard ones. For all of it. I'm not going anywhere."

A tear slips down her cheek, and I reach up to brush it away with my thumb.

"I love you," I say simply. "More than I knew I could love anyone."

Anne sniffles and squeezes my hands. "How am I supposed to follow that?"

A soft ripple of laughter moves through our small audience.

She takes a breath and steadies herself. "Hudson. You are the most stubborn, infuriating, wonderful man I've ever met." That gets another laugh—mostly from Heath. "When we first met, I thought you weren't interested in me at all. You barely said two words."

"I was terrified," I admit.

"I know that now." She smiles. "But even then, there was something about you. Something that made me want to know more. And the more I learned, the more I fell for you."

She steps closer, her voice dropping to something just for us.

"You think you're not good at this—at love, at being part of a family. But Hudson, you're *so* good at it. You just needed someone to see it. And I do. I see you. All of you." She lifts our joined hands and presses a kiss to my knuckles. "I choose you. Today and every day after."

I'm definitely crying now. So is she. So is pretty much everyone in the room, including Heath, who's doing a terrible job of pretending otherwise.

The officiant clears his throat. "Do you, Hudson James Parks, take Anne Elizabeth Masters to be your lawfully wedded wife?"

"I do." The words come out strong and certain.

"And do you, Anne Elizabeth Masters, take Hudson James Parks to be your lawfully wedded husband?"

"I do." Her smile is radiant.

"Then by the power vested in me by the state of Arkansas, I now pronounce you husband and wife." The officiant grins. "You may kiss your bride."

I don't need to be told twice.

I cup her face in my hands and kiss her—soft at first, then deeper when she melts into me. Our families cheer, and I hear Heath let out a whistle that's probably inappropriate for a courthouse, but I don't care.

When we finally break apart, Anne is laughing and crying at the same time.

"We did it," she whispers.

"We did it." I press my forehead to hers. "You're stuck with me now, Mrs. Parks."

"I wouldn't have it any other way."

I take her hand, and together, we turn to face our families—our *family*—as husband and wife.

The future doesn't feel like something to survive.

It feels like something to celebrate.

Bonus Epilogue

FIVE YEARS LATER

GENTLE KISSES ON MY cheeks rouse me from my sleep. "Happy New Year. It's time to get up, babe." Hudson gently rubs my belly. "We have to leave soon for the hospital."

I groan. "I'm scared," I whisper. Today's the day we meet our daughter. She refused to get into the proper position, so we opted for a C-section to make delivery safer for us both.

"I'll be right there with you," Hudson says, helping me sit up. "You're the bravest, most beautiful woman in the world. Have I told you that lately?"

I laugh. "Yes. Every day since you found out I was pregnant."

He kisses me softly. "It's true."

I push to standing and waddle my way into the bathroom. "I'll be ready in five minutes," I say, shutting the door behind me.

I take my time getting ready. These are the last few minutes of solitude before my life changes forever. I've dreamed of being a mom since I was a little kid. Now that it's happening, I realize just how big a responsibility it will be.

The baby kicks, and I hold my hand over my stomach. I can't ever imagine leaving her behind—like Hudson's mom did to him. My heart aches for Hudson, but I'm also angry for him. How could a mother walk away from her child? I don't think I'll ever understand it.

After I finish brushing my teeth and washing my face, I step out into the bedroom and slip on my most comfortable clothes.

"You're sure we have everything?" I ask. Hudson's spent days packing and repacking the bags. "You have the camera and the phone chargers?"

He nods. "I think we're all set." He takes the bags out to the car before coming back inside to get me. "It's strange to think that the next time we come home, we'll have a baby in that car seat."

He helps me into the car, and we're off. Twenty minutes later, we pull up to the hospital, and park. Hudson grabs our bags, and we head inside to the labor and delivery wing. The sun is just coming up over the horizon, and I pause for a minute to take it in.

Once we're inside, we get checked in, and the nurses hook me up to the monitors. The steady rhythm of the baby's heartbeat sounds in the room. "Anesthesia will be here soon to go over your paperwork and get your spinal block in," Briella, our nurse, says.

"Thank you."

When she leaves, Hudson sits gently on the side of the bed and rubs my stomach. "Hi, baby girl, it's your daddy. We're so excited to meet you soon." He leans down and kisses my bulging belly.

Tears leak from the corners of my eyes. Watching him fall in love with our daughter over the last few months has been amazing. We tried for nearly a year before we were successful, and finally, we're about to meet our baby.

"I'm going to miss this," he says, laying his cheek on my stomach where she's currently kicking.

"I'm not," I say. "I can't wait to sleep on my stomach again." Though, truth be told, I think I will miss it. The feel of her in my belly. Having her all to myself. Yeah, I'll miss it.

"We could always have another one," Hudson says. "Or five."

I laugh. "Let's start with one, shall we?"

The anesthesiologist comes in and it's a whirlwind after that. The next thing I know, I'm on the operating table, and the doctor is tugging around.

The operating room is bright and cold, and I'm grateful for the warm blankets the nurses tucked around my upper body. Hudson sits beside my head, his hand wrapped firmly around mine. He's wearing blue scrubs and a surgical cap, and I can't help but think he looks adorable.

"You doing okay?" he asks, his thumb tracing circles on my palm.

"I think so." I can feel tugging and pressure, but no pain. It's the strangest sensation. "Are you?"

He laughs nervously. "I'm trying not to look over the curtain."

"Probably wise."

His eyes meet mine, and I see everything there—the fear, the excitement, the overwhelming love. This man who once told me he'd decided at fifteen that he wasn't meant for relationships. Who kept everyone at arm's length because he was terrified of being left behind.

Now he's here, holding my hand while we wait to meet our daughter.

"I keep thinking about the first time we met," he says softly, leaning closer so only I can hear. "At Heath's birthday party. You were wearing that yellow sundress, and I couldn't stop staring at you."

"You barely said two words to me that night."

"I was terrified." He grins. "You smiled at me and I forgot how to speak."

I squeeze his hand. "And now look at us."

"Now look at us," he echoes, his voice thick with emotion.

The doctor's voice cuts through the moment. "You're going to feel some pressure."

Hudson's grip tightens on my hand. I watch his face as he listens to the sounds beyond the curtain. His jaw is tight, but his eyes never leave mine.

"I love you," he whispers. "No matter what happens, I need you to know that. You changed everything for me, Anne. Everything."

Before I can respond, the doctor speaks again.

"Almost there," she says. "Okay, here's baby. We've got a little foot here, and there's the other. Oh, and here she comes! She's out. The cord is short, so give us a minute." I feel a weird sensation of movement, and then I hear it—our daughter's first cry.

Tears are flowing freely from my eyes and down toward my ears. Being flat on my back has some drawbacks, but when the doctor lifts her over the curtain, I can't help but fall completely and utterly in love with the tiniest human being I've ever seen.

"She's perfect, Mom." The doctor hands her to a nurse, who dries her off and gently lays her on my chest. Hudson pulls his chair next to us and we get three perfect minutes looking at her eyes, her mouth, her tiny body. Kissing her sweet head. The nurse appears again with a fresh swaddle blanket and wraps her up, then takes her to get her measurements. The doctor says, "Dad, want to follow them and cut the cord?"

Hudson jumps up from his seat. "Yes!" He leans down and kisses my cheek. "You okay?"

"Go," I tell him. "Stay with her. I'll be fine."

I lose sight of what's happening, but Hudson calls out all of her stats like a sports commentator at a recruiting event. "She's twenty and a half inches long."

The doctor chuckles. "You're almost closed up and then we'll get you to recovery where you can hold her, okay?"

"Thank you," I say, listening to her soft cries from across the room.

"Babe, she's huge!" Hudson calls. "Eight pounds, five ounces. Isn't that big?" The nurse tells him that's on the large side of average and he scoffs. "Don't listen to her, sweetheart. You're Daddy's strong girl, aren't you?"

"We're going to take her to the nursery and get her cleaned up and then we'll bring her to you, okay?" Briella says, holding her to me so I can see her precious face. "It will only be a few minutes, I promise."

I kiss her little cheek and fight back tears. It's hard to be stuck on this table when I want to be holding her close to me.

"Do you want me to stay with you?" Hudson asks, looking torn as could be when he notices the tears in my eyes.

"No, go with her."

He nods and kisses me quickly. "I love you."

"I love you, too."

Two hours later, I'm in a private room and the baby is nestled against my chest in a milk coma when our parents come into the room. "There she is," Lori, Hudson's step-mom says, stepping up to the bed. "She's so precious, isn't she, Jake?"

Jake grins up at Hudson. "Your life just changed forever, son." He melts into a puddle of goo when she makes a little squeaking noise.

"Don't I know it," Hudson says, but he's grinning like a fool. He hasn't stopped grinning since they placed her on my chest.

Jake claps him on the shoulder, and I catch the shine of tears in his eyes. "I'm so proud of you," he says quietly.

Hudson's throat bobs as he swallows hard. "Thanks, Dad."

Lori wraps an arm around Jake's waist and leans into him. "We're both so proud," she adds. "And we're going to spoil this little one rotten. Fair warning."

"Get in line," my mom says, finally pulling her gaze away from Ophelia's sleeping face. "I've already started a collection of children's books. The classics. Goodnight Moon, Where the Wild Things Are, The Velveteen Rabbit . . ."

"She's not even a day old and she already has a library," Dad chuckles.

"A child can never have too many books," Mom says primly.

I watch my parents crowd around the bassinet, their faces soft with wonder. Dad's got his arm around Mom's shoulders, and she's leaning into him the same way Lori leans into Jake. Two couples, decades of love between them, united by this tiny new person.

"She has your nose," Mom tells me. "And Hudson's chin, I think."

"Poor kid," Hudson jokes, rubbing his jaw.

"Hush," Lori says. "She's perfect."

Jake moves closer to get a better look, and Ophelia chooses that exact moment to yawn—a huge, dramatic yawn that scrunches up her entire face. The room erupts in soft laughter.

"Oh, she's got personality already," Jake says. "Just like her daddy."

"I was a very calm baby, thank you very much," Hudson protests.

Jake snorts. "You screamed for the first three months of your life. Your mother and I took shifts just to survive."

The mention of Hudson's mother sends a brief ripple through the room. I see Hudson's shoulders tense, just slightly, before Lori smoothly redirects.

"Well, I'm sure Ophelia will be an angel," she says. "Look at that sweet face."

I catch Hudson's eye and offer him a small smile. He returns it, and I watch the tension ease from his posture. We've talked about his mom, the hurt and the scars that still linger. But we've also talked about breaking the cycle. About being present. Choosing to stay.

He chose me. He chose us. And watching him now, surrounded by family, I know he's exactly where he's meant to be.

"Let's give them some room." Lori leads Jake to the back of the room, and my parents step close to my bed.

"My baby had a baby," Mom says, giving me a watery grin. She leans in and places a kiss on my forehead. "You did good," she whispers, taking it all in.

"What'd you decide to name her?" Dad asks, running his finger along her perfect little hand.

Hudson looks over at me, and I smile back at him. "You tell them, babe. It was your idea."

He nods and comes to stand by me, resting his hand on her little back.

"Meet Ophelia Grace Parks," he says, his voice soft so as to not disturb her, "the love of our lives."

"It's a perfect name," Mom says. "Can I hold her?"

I shift, and Mom carefully takes her from the bassinet. "Oh, she's so sweet. Nanny loves you already, little one." She sways gently, with Ophelia in her arms.

"Okay," Dad says, reaching out for her. "My turn."

After the grandparents all get a turn to hold her, they say goodbye and ease the door shut behind them, leaving us alone as a family of three. Hudson takes Ophelia and holds her to his chest. The sight of my big strong husband caring for her so sweetly does something to me I can't explain, and suddenly the idea of more babies doesn't seem so scary.

I shift in bed and wince.

Then again, I haven't even begun to heal from this one.

"We're parents," Hudson whispers. "We're a family."

I nod. "We are."

"Can you believe we made her?" he asks, his voice filled with awe.

"I did most of the work," I tease.

He laughs softly and sways gently from side to side, cradling her in his arms. "She's so small. How is she so small?"

"She didn't feel small a few hours ago."

He winces sympathetically. "Fair point."

He cradles her against his chest, one large hand supporting her head, and I watch his whole body soften.

"I used to think I'd never have this," he says quietly, his eyes fixed on her face. "A wife. A baby. A family." He shakes his head slowly. "I convinced myself I didn't want it. That I was better off alone."

"What changed?"

He looks up at me, and the love in his eyes nearly takes my breath away. "You. You changed everything." He pauses, gathering his thoughts. "The night I walked you to your car at McFadden's—do you remember that?"

"Of course I do."

"I almost kissed you." A rueful smile tugs at his lips. "I wanted to so badly. But I was scared. Scared of what it would mean if I let myself feel something real."

I reach out and rest my hand on his knee. "And now?"

"Now I can't imagine my life without you." He looks back down at Ophelia, and his voice drops to a whisper. "Without either of you."

Ophelia stirs in his arms, her tiny fingers curling and uncurling against his chest. He lifts her gently and presses a kiss to her forehead.

"I'm going to be here," he tells her, his voice fierce and tender all at once. "Every day. Every scraped knee and bad dream and broken heart. I'm not going anywhere. I promise you that."

Tears prick at my eyes. I know he's not just talking to her. He's making a vow—to both of us, and maybe to himself.

He rises from the chair and gently lays her in the bassinet before coming to me and placing a soft kiss on my lips. "I never knew I could be this happy," Hudson says softly.

As I gaze into his eyes, filled with hope and love, I realize that wishes really can come true.

If you loved this story, I'd appreciate if you left a review! They are so helpful to authors and fellow readers. Even a star rating helps.

Curious about the bachelor auction Mrs. Willowby is planning? Download the exclusive newsletter bonus and find out!

Want to keep in touch? Join my newsletter at tiamarlee.com/newsletter and never miss a new release!

The first book in the Piney Brook Wishes series is *His Christmas Wish*. If you started the series late, now's the time to go back to the beginning and fall in love with Morgan and Brant.

If you love small-town, ranch family romances, check out *His to Have*.

About the author

Tia Marlee enjoys delivering swoon worthy HEA's in her clean and wholesome romance novels. A small-town girl at heart, Tia's stories have that small-town, Hallmark charm with a dash of real life, and a laugh thrown in for good measure.

Tia is the author of the Piney Book Wishes series featuring unexpected love stories based in small-town Piney Brook, Arkansas. She's also proud to be part of the multi-author romcom series The Coffee Loft season one and two.

Tia resides in Texas with her husband and three teenaged children. When she's not writing or reading, you can find her standing barefoot in her front yard, loving on her 80 pound lap dog, or hauling kids from one activity to the next.

Let's Stay In Touch

YOU CAN FIND ME at my website: https://tiamarlee.com
Follow me:
Facebook: https://tinyurl.com/FBTiaMarlee
Instagram: https://tinyurl.com/IGTiaMarlee
Amazon: https://tinyurl.com/AmazonTiaMarlee
BookBub: https://tinyurl.com/BBTiaMarlee
Goodreads: https://tinyurl.com/GRTiaMarlee

Join my reader group: https://tinyurl.com/TiaMarleeReaderGroup

Also By Tia Marlee

Piney Brook Wishes Series
His Christmas Wish
Sweet Summertime Wishes
Wishing for the Girl Next Door
A Soldier's Wish
Her New Year's Wish
The Piney Brook Wishes Box Set

Standalones in the Piney Brook Wishes World
Sunkissed By My Best Friend
Wishing for Forever

The Coffee Loft Series
Bean Wishing for a Latte Love
You Mocha Me Crazy
A Brewtiful Kind of Love
Coffee Loft Collection

Apple Blossom Ranch Series

His to Adore
His to Have
His to Hold
His to Love
His to Cherish
Hers to Treasure

Sugar and Sirens
Still Yours, Always Mine
Catch Me, If You Can
Sweeter With You
A Little Bit Married
The Last First Kiss

A Little Bit of Christmas
Merry & Bright: The Great Light Fight
Gnome Sweet Home
The Candy Cane Parade
Mistletoe at Midnight